DOCTOR WHO AND THE
MASQUE OF MANDRAGORA

CW00953129

DOCTOR WHO AND THE MASQUE OF MANDRAGORA

Based on the BBC television serial *The Masque of Mandragora* by Louis Marks by arrangement with the British Broadcasting Corporation

PHILIP HINCHCLIFFE

published by
the Paperback Division of
W. H. ALLEN & CO. LTD

A Target Book
Published in 1977
by the Paperback Division of W. H. Allen & Co. Ltd
A Howard & Wyndham Company
44 Hill Street, London W1X 8LB

Reprinted 1979
Reprinted 1982

Novelisation copyright © 1977 by Philip Hinchcliffe
Original script copyright © 1976 by Louis Marks
'Doctor Who' series copyright © 1976, 1977 by the
British Broadcasting Corporation

Printed in Great Britain by
Cox & Wyman Ltd, Reading

ISBN 0 426 11893 6

Contents

1 The Mandragora Helix   7

2 The Brethren of Demnos   15

3 Execution!   26

4 Sacrifice   35

5 The Prince Must Die   46

6 The Secret of the Temple   51

7 The Spell of Evil   59

8 Torture!   70

9 The Invasion Begins   84

10 Siege   94

11 Duel to the Death   106

12 The Final Eclipse   115

The Mandragora Helix

The year was 1492, the place—a remote principality in Northern Italy. A handful of ragged peasants sweated and strained as they hauled a cart full of hay along a steep path. Their faces were lined and careworn by years of drudgery but their natural high spirits remained undimmed as they swore and cajoled amongst themselves with great gusto.

They reached the brow of the hill and paused for breath. Suddenly the air was filled with the pounding of horses' hooves and a troop of armed men appeared, their helmets and breastplates glinting in the sun. Swiftly they surrounded the defenceless peasants. One of them brandished a burning torch. With a grin he tossed it into the cart. The dry grass exploded into flame. Terrified, the peasants began screaming and running in all directions. The horsemen allowed them to get a short distance away then drew their swords and started to ride them down. As each peasant was caught he was mercilessly butchered.

The slaughter continued for several minutes until a harsh voice rang out.

'Leave a few alive, Captain, to tell the others how insurrection is dealt with!'

The captain of the troop saluted and called his men off. The man who gave the order was seated astride a majestic ebony-black stallion. The man wore rich and elaborate clothes denoting he was someone of rank and power, a hunting outfit in red velvet covered by a black silken cloak. But this outward elegance was marred by his own features which were brutal and ugly: heavy-lidded eyes, dark and cold, a nose hooked like a vulture's beak, a mouth set in a permanent sneer.

Apparently pleased with the scene of bloodshed and carnage, he wheeled his horse and spurred it savagely in the ribs. The animal darted forward at a gallop and the troop of horsemen fell in behind and followed.

'Make way! Make way for Count Federico!'

The mounted troop thundered through the city gates scattering all before them and pulled up inside the palace courtyard. The Count dismounted and, with a quick glance towards a large shuttered window, entered the palace.

Behind the shutters a sombre drama was being enacted. The old Duke of San Martino—a feared but just ruler—lay dying. Around his deathbed were gathered all his courtiers, grave and respectful. By the old man's pillow, clasping his thin bony hand, knelt a young man of about twenty. He was strikingly handsome with long, dark-brown hair. This was his son and heir Giuliano. The young Prince fought bravely to control his emotions as the priest administered the Last Rites.

Observing the scene, a few paces removed, was the bizarre figure of the court astrologer, Hieronymous. His eyes darted ceaselessly round the room like a trapped bird of prey. His long thick beard, black skull cap and voluminous cloak gave him a strange and sinister appearance. Even those who knew him well felt uneasy in his presence.

Abruptly the priest's low mumblings came to a halt. It was over. The Duke was dead. Giuliano rose and looked down on his father's face, austere and imposing

8

even in this last moment of life. A tall blond young man touched his arm in comfort. It was his childhood friend and companion Marco.

'He was a good man, Giuliano. A just and noble ruler.'

Giuliano nodded then turned round and faced the astrologer. 'Hieronymous, you foretold my father's death. How?'

'Everything is foretold by the stars,' replied the old soothsayer gravely. 'I am just a humble astrologer, I only interpret their meaning.'

'But the exact day—the very hour—it's not possible.' The young Prince clenched his fist in disbelief.

'When Mars comes into conjunction with Saturn in the seventh layer, and the moon is full-grown . . . death comes to great ones. So it is decreed.' The astrologer raised his arms heavenwards and turned to leave.

As he reached the doors Count Federico entered. A look of understanding passed between them unnoticed by anyone else in the room, then the astrologer swept out.

'I'm sorry you could not be present at my father's deathbed, Uncle,' said Giuliano bitingly.

'I came as soon as I could. There were important matters of state to attend to.'

'I see. I'm sorry. I thought you were out enjoying some sport.'

The Count's eyes flashed with anger. 'There was trouble among the peasants. They needed teaching a lesson.' He rapped his thigh with a leather riding whip.

Giuliano smiled sarcastically. 'Isn't that your sport, Uncle?'

The Count stared hatefully at his nephew for a moment then turned on his heel and stalked out.

'You are upset my lord,' said Marco soothingly, 'but

do not anger your uncle—not at this time.' He dropped his voice, 'Remember he is strong and ruthless.'

Giuliano drew himself up proudly—his handsome face stern and regal. 'I am Duke now. I want to rule over a land where there is no tyranny, no blind ignorance and superstition like that old fool Hieronymous preaches. We make our own lives, not the stars.'

Marco nodded in agreement. 'Nevertheless it is most remarkable. Your father was in good health. To be struck down so suddenly ... and Hieronymous did predict it exactly.'

Far and deep in the Space–Time Vortex a strange blue craft blinked and shimmered like a shaft of light. The craft was unusually shaped, about eight feet high and five feet square and on its top flashed a small white lamp. It had an altogether enigmatic and alien appearance. Unless, that is, you happened to be an earthling from the mid-twentieth century. In which case you would have recognised it as a very ordinary London police box. But even then you would have been misled. Because inside, the craft was infinitely larger than it was on the outside, and looked nothing like a police box. In fact it bore far more resemblance to a highly sophisticated space ship, which is what it was. A ship which travelled through Space and Time! Its inner workings embodied a secret which had eluded countless civilisations since the dawn of life itself.

The owner of the ship, however, seemed quite at home with this grandiose achievement and frequently complained when things went wrong. At this moment he was striding purposefully along one of the many gleaming white corridors which ran off the main control room. He was a tall curly-haired man of indeterminate age with sparkling blue eyes and a beaming smile. He was dressed rather curiously in tweed trousers and a long red-velvet frockcoat. Round his neck he wore a very long woollen scarf of many colours which trailed on the ground behind him.

By his side was a pretty young woman who kept asking questions as they walked along the corridor. She was Sarah Jane Smith, a London journalist who had first met the Doctor several years before when he had visited Earth. She had accompanied him on other adventures since, and now felt she knew him well. Even so the Doctor was always surprising her with something novel and unexpected. This was the first time, for example, he had allowed her to really explore the TARDIS.

She gazed round in fascination at the white walls with their weird hexagonal indentations. They seemed to glow with an unearthly light.

'I've never been in this section before,' she said admiringly.

'One day I'll give you a proper guided tour,' replied the Doctor. 'If I can remember the way.' He stopped by an open doorway. Sarah peered in. A vast room stretched out before her, empty apart from a pair of shoes in the middle of the floor.

'What's this?'

'Boot cupboard. Not very interesting.' The Doctor pressed a button and the door closed.

Sarah frowned. 'Doctor?'

'Mmmm?'

'Just how big *is* the TARDIS?'

The Doctor shrugged. 'How big is big? Relative dimensions, you see. No constant.' He continued walking.

'That's not an answer.'

The Doctor stopped and turned. 'All right—how big are you? At the moment?'

Sarah drew herself up to her full height, which wasn't very tall. 'Five feet five and a quarter.'

'Bah!' snorted the Doctor. 'There are no measurements in infinity. You humans have such little minds. I don't know why I like you.' He strode off again. Sarah was not sure whether he was really cross or not. She was about to tell him not to be so rude when her attention was caught by a recess in the wall. She pressed a button and the wall slid open to reveal a room beyond.

'Hey what's this place?'

Inside it was dark and dusty. The walls were panelled just like the main control room but in brown mahogany not white. In the centre stood a hexagonal console, a smaller more old-fashioned version of the one Sarah knew.

'This is the secondary control centre,' said the Doctor appearing in the doorway. 'I can run the TARDIS just as easily from here as from the old one.' He thought for a moment. 'Come to think of it this *was* the old one. Let's see now.' He pressed some coloured switches on the console. There was a humming noise and a section of one wall slid back to reveal a monitor screen. It showed a twisting swirling whirlpool of stars, formed into a giant spiral. At the same instant the TARDIS began to judder and sway.

'Oh dear!' said the Doctor unhappily.

'Something wrong?'

'It's the Mandragora Helix. I thought we'd avoided it. I should have known better than to cut through uncharted segments of the Vortex.' He started to punch buttons furiously on the console. 'Let's hope we can counter-magnetise enough to resist the pull.'

Sarah frowned. 'What is the Mandragora Helix, Doctor?'

'A spiral of pure energy radiating outwards in ways

12

we don't fully understand—except that at its centre there is a controlling intelligence.'

'An intelligence? You mean something living?'

'Oh, certainly living—in its fashion. But that's all anyone's ever established.'

The room began to shake more severely and a loud shrieking noise howled around them.

'It's sucking us in!' yelled Sarah.

'We'll have to thrust straight through and hope we come out the other side,' shouted the Doctor as the sound increased.

Sarah began to stagger. The shrieking was becoming unbearable. 'It's getting into my head!' she cried.

'Concentrate Sarah! Keep your mind on something —anything!'

'I can't!'

'Say the alphabet backwards. Go on. Z ... Y ... X ...'

Sarah pressed her hands to her ears and forced herself to concentrate. '... W ... V ... U ... T ...'

The room began to spin and topple. They were now in the very eye of the Helix and plunging faster and faster to the bottom of the whirlpool. The noise was like the screeching of souls in torment. The Doctor wrestled with the controls but the violent motions of the TARDIS hurled him to the floor. The room seemed to buckle and split like a distorted mirror-image of itself and the noise intensified to an excruciating pitch.

Then suddenly the sensation died away and everything fell quiet and still.

'... F ... E ... D ... C ... B ... A!' Sarah opened her eyes triumphantly.

The Doctor smiled at her from the floor. 'No ill effects?'

'I don't think so. Are we there?'

'Where?'

'Where we were going.'

The Doctor scrambled to his feet and examined the console. 'Hard to say. The astrosextant rectifier has gone out of phase. No other damage though.' He beamed brightly. 'I'll just pop out and see where we are. Stay here.'

The Doctor stepped out from the TARDIS and looked around. They had landed inside a circle of mountainous crystals which seemed to hang in the air like magic. As he looked the Doctor realised that beyond the first circle of crystals was a second, and a third, and a fourth, and so on into infinity. It was impossible to tell how near or far away they were. For a moment he felt he could almost reach out his hand and touch them. Then suddenly they were like distant mountain ranges and the TARDIS a tiny speck on the shimmering plain between.

'I see what you mean about relative dimensions,' said a voice at his elbow.

'I thought I told you to stay ...' Before the Doctor could finish Sarah grabbed his sleeve.

'Sssh! What's that noise?'

A rushing rumbling sound like an approaching hurricane filled their ears. A look of alarm spread across the Doctor's face.

'Mandragora Energy!' he whispered. 'Quick—get down!' He threw an arm round Sarah and pulled her to safety behind a corner of the TARDIS. The air grew hot and red and a ball of blazing light seemed to envelop them and the TARDIS. Then, just as swiftly, it disappeared and the roaring wind faded to a distant moan.

'That could have been very nasty,' said the Doctor quietly. 'Come on. I think we'd better get out of here.' He paused. 'That is, if they will allow us to.' He bun-

14

dled Sarah through the open door of the TARDIS and
slammed it shut.

Within a few seconds the familiar white light began
to flash and the TARDIS dematerialised. As it vanished a rumble of triumphant laughter echoed around
the crystal mountains like a clap of thunder.

2

The Brethren of Demnos

'He angers me! The last obstacle between myself and
the Dukedom.'

Count Federico spat out the words with venom as
he paced the chamber of Hieronymous, the court
astrologer. The room was small and dark, crammed
with old charts, astrolobes, ancient books and bottled
potions—all the paraphernalia of astromancy. Hieronymous was tending a noxious substance bubbling inside a large brass cauldron.

'You mean your nephew, Giuliano?' replied the
cunning soothsayer. He knew very well whom the
Count had in mind.

'Yes, yes. How soon will he die?'

Hieronymous continued to stir his foul concoction.
'You must be patient.'

The Count snorted. 'I have been patient. Now the
Dukedom is almost in my grasp.' He curled his gloved
hand in a crushing gesture.

'Nevertheless,' the sorcerer went on craftily, 'so many
deaths in so short a time . . . all so sudden.'

'But you said yourself it was written in the stars.' A
sneer spread over the Count's ugly features. 'Don't say

you are doubting your own prophecies?'

The sorcerer's eyes flashed momentarily with anger. 'Giuliano has a sharp mind. He may suspect.'

'All the more reason to act quickly. A day—two days at the most. You have the poison still ready?'

Hieronymous did not reply but crossed to the casement window and gazed out, a faraway look in his eyes.

'Well? What's wrong?' the Count grew restless.

'These last few weeks as the summer solstice approaches I've felt ...' Hieronymous turned and paused. 'You wouldn't understand ...'

'Go on, go on.'

'I've felt as if my powers were growing, as if I had been chosen to be granted visions of the future.'

'Hah!' the Count scoffed. 'So many correct predictions have gone to your head.'

'The stars will not be mocked!' cried the astrologer fiercely.

'And neither will I!' thundered the Count equally aroused. 'Cast your horoscope, soothsayer. The young Duke Giuliano will die suddenly in two days' time. I will do the rest!' He swept angrily out of the room.

Hieronymous tugged on his beard for a moment deep in thought, then crossed to the window once more. As he stared at the sky a clap of thunder echoed across the heavens like an omen from the gods.

The Doctor opened the door of the TARDIS and peered out.

'That's strange. A forced landing.'

They appeared to be wedged in a very large bush overhanging a slope.

'You mean you weren't in control?' enquired Sarah

sweetly, knowing how touchy the Doctor was on this subject.

The Doctor scowled and scrambled out. Sarah followed with more difficulty.

'It's very pleasant,' she said when her feet finally touched the ground and she could look around properly. 'Ooh look, grapes!' She set off to explore.

They had landed in a vineyard on the side of a hill. The climate was warm and sunny and Sarah delightedly stuffed her mouth full of grapes. 'Delicious!' she shouted, 'and just look at those peaches over there.' She ran off up the slope.

The Doctor seemed not to hear. 'Perhaps that's the reason I stopped using the old control room?' he muttered to himself puzzled. He gave up the problem and looked about him.

A piece of broken glass caught his eye on the ground a few feet away. He bent down and studied it.

'Hmm. Earth, Mediterranean, late fifteenth-century Italian.' He tossed it to one side. 'Not a pleasant period. I think we'll be on our way.' He stood up and looked round for Sarah. She was nowhere to be seen.

'Sarah! Where are you?'

The Doctor's voice carried faintly over the hill to where Sarah was now happily picking peaches. She gave a little grin but didn't reply.

Less than ten paces away three hooded figures in black robes were carefully watching her every move. Oblivious to the danger Sarah drew nearer and nearer the hidden watchers. She began to hum a tune. Suddenly she heard a noise.

'Is that you, Doct . . .' The words froze on her lips as the hooded assailants lunged towards her. Before she could speak one of them clamped a large hand over her mouth. The next moment she was being dragged away roughly through the bushes. She tried to struggle but the hand over her mouth was stopping her breath. Her lungs felt ready to burst and the blood rushed to her head.

They must have covered about a hundred yards when a voice rang out from behind them. 'Stop!'

Sarah's captors turned to see the imposing figure of the Doctor advancing towards them. The largest of them ran to attack the Doctor but as he got within arm's length he was suddenly lifted off his feet and hurled through the air in a graceful arc. He landed heavily on the hard earth with a grunt and rolled over apparently unconscious.

'Now put her down,' commanded the Doctor to the other two. Gingerly they lowered Sarah's inert form to the ground.

'Right. Move away.' The two hooded figures obeyed. 'Good.' The Doctor stepped forward to examine Sarah but as he did so there was a flash of action behind him and a heavy stone crashed mercilessly against the back of his head. He fell like a log.

The third figure stepped over the Doctor's crumpled body and dropped the stone with which he had dealt the vicious blow. Swiftly and silently, the three of them lifted Sarah up again and disappeared with their bundle into the dark woods nearby.

A hundred yards away the TARDIS stood alone and unguarded, partly hidden among the vines. All at once the door started to open slowly of its own accord and a blazing obelisk of fiery red light emerged. It was accompanied by a rushing shrieking sound which startled all the birds and sent them squawking away in panic. The ball of light hovered for a few seconds outside the TARDIS then set off gradually through the trees about three feet above the ground. As it

18

moved it left a darkened trail of burnt and shrivelled foliage.

The Doctor slowly recovered consciousness and clambered to his feet. A sharp stabbing pain in the back of his head reminded him all too clearly of what had occurred. He shouted Sarah's name but she and the hooded figures had vanished. He wondered what to do next—everything was a disagreeable mystery.

He was standing on a narrow footpath which led into a thick wood. He decided he had no recourse but to follow it.

The path ran steeply down between mossy banks and overhanging trees and then levelled off after half a mile and came to a small lake. On the opposite side was a peasant gathering rushes. He had already laid some on the bank to dry, and was now tossing them into a cart with a pitchfork.

The Doctor was on the point of calling out to him when he heard a strange screeching sound overhead. He glanced up and saw what looked like a red fireball swooping down towards the lake from out of the sky. As he watched, it plunged beneath the water's surface and headed towards the peasant leaving a hissing bubbling trail in its wake. The peasant was paralysed with fright. He clutched his pitchfork in self-defence but before he could move the glowing phosphorescence rose out of the water and engulfed him in a sizzling flash.

It was all over in a matter of seconds. The Doctor hurried to where the peasant had fallen. All that remained was a blackened corpse.

'Mandragora Energy!' whispered the Doctor, horrified. 'It must have got into the TARDIS.'

Grimly he studied the trail of smouldering grass indicating the passage of the lethal bolt. He shuddered at the thought of what further destruction this evil and irresistible force might wreak. Whatever its purpose one fact was irrefutable. He, the Doctor, was the unwitting cause of the death he had just witnessed. It was he who had brought this deadly menace to Earth. And at the moment he had no idea how to combat it.

Giuliano was seated at a table in his private chamber in the palace. With him was Marco. Instead of their usual silken doublet and hose both men wore the official clothes of mourning. The face of the young Prince was pallid and wan but now and then a flicker of life crossed his features as he toyed with various round pieces of glass on the table in front of him. Eventually he took one up and fitted it inside a rudimentary-looking telescope.

'There's a man in Florence,' he said squinting through the eye-piece, 'who claims that by arranging ground glasses in certain orders it is possible to see the moon and stars as large as your hand.'

Marco looked up from cleaning his sword. 'Is that a good thing?'

'Of course it's a good thing. That way we can find out more about them.'

Marco tossed back his blond hair and smiled. 'What is there to know about the stars except how they move in the heavens? And we've known that for hundreds of years.'

'That's the whole point, Marco,' exclaimed Giuliano excitedly, jumping up from the table. 'Perhaps they don't move as we think they move. That's what this man in Florence is saying. Perhaps it is we who move!'

Before Marco could respond the door to the chamber burst open and Count Federico strode in followed by Hieronymous in his skullcap and trailing robes. Giuliano's animated mood was immediately dispelled.

'It is customary to knock before entering a room, Uncle,' he said coolly.

'I'm sorry,' replied Federico without appearing so, 'but there is bad news, Giuliano.'

For a moment the young Duke looked fearful. 'Why? What's happened?'

Federico motioned the soothsayer forward. 'Tell him.'

Hieronymous bowed obsequiously. 'Sire, forgive me, it is not of my doing—but this morning I was casting a horoscope——'

'I've told you often enough,' interrupted Giuliano, 'I don't believe in horoscopes.'

Hieronymous shook his head sadly. 'I only wish I too could not believe. But it was there too plainly to be ignored . . .' He broke off.

'What was there?'

'I cannot speak of it,' whispered the astrologer, clearly overcome by the dire nature of his premonition. Giuliano began to grasp the meaning of this charade.

'My death?' he scoffed.

'Please, my lord. Do not take these things lightly.' Hieronymous's face wore a pained expression. He leant forward and took hold of Giuliano's arm. 'I beg you not to leave the palace on any account. Take no risks of any kind. Perhaps it can be . . . avoided.' He stared into the young Duke's eyes.

Giuliano seemed unmoved. 'I have no intention of sacrificing my life to satisfy some old superstitious nonsense.'

Hieronymous glanced at Federico. The Count stepped forward. His long nose and raven black hair poked out from beneath a black velvet hat making him look more sinister than ever. 'Remember your father, Giuliano. He, too, scoffed.'

'Yes, I remember my father,' replied the young Duke tight-lipped. 'His death remains a mystery. But it was nothing to do with the stars, of that I am certain.' He stared straight at Federico who was forced to turn away beneath his unflinching gaze.

'And how are the troubles with the peasants, Uncle?' Giuliano continued after a moment, this time in a mocking tone.

'We think they are being stirred up by spies sent from our enemies,' Federico smiled coldly, 'but we shall catch them—and make them pay for it.' He slapped his gloved palm with his riding whip and, motioning Hieronymous to follow stalked out of the room.

Giuliano and Marco exchanged worried glances. There was intrigue and villainy afoot.

The Doctor hurried on through the wood. He had abandoned the futile search on foot for the Mandragora Energy. His foremost concern now was to recover Sarah.

He rounded a bend in a path and came upon a group of peasants resting beneath a tree. He extracted a peach from his pocket and, taking a bite, approached the peasants in a nonchalant manner.

'Excuse me, I'm a traveller in these parts. I was wondering if you had happened to see ...' He broke off aware of a sudden panic in their faces. In an instant the peasants had snatched up their belongings and fled into the woods leaving him quite alone. The reason for their flight was quickly explained as a troop of armed soldiers rode up and surrounded the Doctor. They were attired in yellow and scarlet livery.

The captain of the troop, a heavily built man with a scar on his left cheek, addressed the Doctor rudely. 'Who are you?'

'I'm a traveller.'

'Where from?'

The Doctor smiled. 'My dear fellow, you'd never believe me. By the way you haven't seen a young girl have you? About five feet five and ...'

'Silence!' the captain roared at him.

'... probably got peach juice all over her chin ...'

The captain whipped out his sword and held it to the Doctor's throat. 'Your life is in peril, dog! Produce your documents.'

The Doctor raised an eyebrow. 'Documents? Certainly—hold this for a moment.' He pushed the sword aside and stabbed his peach on the point. The captain, taken aback, was momentarily speechless.

'I think you'll find some of these rather interesting,' said the Doctor, rummaging around in his pockets. He pulled out a large football rattle and stared at it with vague surprise. 'Extraordinary the things one carries about one's person.' He suddenly whirled the rattle in front of the captain's horse. The animal shied and reared, unseating its rider.

'After him!' yelled the captain, struggling to get his breath back.

But the Doctor was already doubling between the stationary horses like a hare in flight. Before anyone could move he had pulled a soldier from his mount, leapt into the saddle and spurred the animal away down the path. In the confusion it took several seconds for the remaining soldiers to gather their wits and set off in pursuit. This they eventually did with the scar-faced captain bellowing angry imprecations at their rear.

It was a long time since the Doctor had ridden a horse. Luckily the animal was strong and surefooted and gradually they began to draw clear of their pursuers. The Doctor had no idea where he was heading. At some point he knew he would have to leave the main path and set off into the woodland if he were to lose his trackers completely.

He rounded a bend and came to a fork in the path. Approaching him from the left was a large body of mounted soldiers in the same scarlet and yellow livery. He wheeled his horse to the right and set off down the clear pathway but too late saw it was a trap. Above him in a large overhanging tree were two soldiers waiting to pounce. As his horse passed beneath they dropped like stones onto the Doctor's back and hurled him to the ground. The Doctor let out a cry of pain as his head caught a sharp rock. The force of the blow knocked him unconscious and he lay there dishevelled and defenceless as the pursuing captain and his troop arrived on the scene.

The captain grunted with satisfaction as he observed the Doctor's prostrate form. 'Bind the dog before he recovers his wits!' he ordered. 'Count Federico will want to question this one!'

Sarah woke to find herself tied and gagged. Two men were bundling her through a warren of dark stone passages. She guessed they must be underground because the air was damp and chill and the only source of light came from burning torches set at intervals in the walls. She realised she must have lost consciousness when the hooded figures smothered her in the woods. She had no idea how far they had come, and still had not seen the faces of her kidnappers. They kept their black cowls well forward like monks.

Presently they entered a vast underground chamber like a huge cavern scooped out of a rocky hillside. More of the hooded figures formed a semi-circle around a rectangular stone altar in the middle of the chamber. One of them stepped forward as she was dragged in. This time she could see his face, he made no attempt to hide it. He was tall and hollow-cheeked, a fanatical gleam in his eyes.

'Release her,' he said. His voice sounded reverential and priestly but Sarah felt sure this was not a Christian sect. The whole place smelt of occultism and magic.

'Where was she found?'

'On the slopes of the Hill of Sorrows.'

'At what hour?'

'At the noon hour.'

The priestly one nodded with satisfaction. 'Exactly as it was foretold. A maiden of face and sturdy of body.'

'You can forget the flattery,' said Sarah as her gag was removed. 'What do you want?'

The voice grew more incantatory. 'It is written that some are conscious of the purpose for which they are chosen, others are as innocent as lambs.'

'Sorry?' replied Sarah not following his drift. 'Try again.'

'My child, the purity of your sacrifice renders it doubly welcome to the mighty Demnos, god of the twin realms of moontide and solstice.'

'Sacrifice? Now just a minute——' Their intention was now becoming very clear. The priest ignored her. Raising his voice he commanded, 'Let her be prepared to receive the sacrificial blade!'

25

Before Sarah could protest the two hooded brothers grabbed her arms and began to drag her across the floor of the chamber.

3

Execution!

The Doctor came round. His head was muzzy and throbbed with pain. His mind struggled to focus itself. He was being half carried across a smooth marble floor. Sounds echoed loudly as if they were in a long corridor. Every so often a large stone pillar brushed past his shoulder. It dawned on him that he was inside some sort of palace.

His captors stopped outside a pair of heavy ornate doors which swung open before them like magic. They entered. Inside was a large and richly furnished state-room. In the centre flanked by guards in scarlet livery sat an imposing figure on a raised throne. He was elegantly dressed in silk and ermine robes, on his head the black velvet hat emphasised the coarseness of his face beneath. The Doctor noted the vulture-like nose and thin-lipped mouth and decided it was not a face he could readily warm to.

'This is the man, sire,' said a voice at the Doctor's elbow and he was thrust roughly forward. The Doctor recognised the voice as belonging to the scar-faced captain.

'So!' Count Federico rose to his feet and studied the Doctor. 'I hear you led my ruffians quite a dance.'

The Doctor smiled. 'Just a short gallop. Good for the liver.'

'What is your name?'

'Doctor will do.'

The Count fingered the Doctor's coat. 'You wear strange garments. Where are you from?'

'Does it matter?' responded the Doctor rudely.

The Count's features contorted themselves into an even uglier expression. 'You are tall enough, Doctor. Answer my questions civilly and promptly or your body will be lengthened on the rack.'

'Don't threaten me,' replied the Doctor sharply. 'I've come here to help you.'

The captain stepped forward ready to strike. 'Sire, let me punish the insolent dog!'

'Wait!' the Count waved him back. 'The fellow puzzles me.' He stared curiously at the Doctor. 'What help do I need?'

The Doctor leant closer to explain. 'An energy wave —part of the Mandragora Helix—has been released here. It could do untold damage. It must be neutralised immediately.'

Federico scowled. 'What language is this? Make yourself plain.'

The Doctor looked round the circle of uncomprehending faces. He'd forgotten he was in the fifteenth century. 'Let me put it this way—a ball of heavenly fire has come to Earth and will consume all who stand in its path. I must take it back to the stars.'

There was a stunned silence then a ripple of laughter ran through the room. The captain spoke first. 'His mind is afflicted, sire, the fall from the horse ...'

'No,' said the Count with a glint of understanding in his eyes. 'He professes sorcery.' He smiled evilly at the Doctor. 'But there is no gold for you in San Martino. My seer, Hieronymous, is the finest in the land.'

'Well just ask your seer if he's ever seen an energy wave,' replied the Doctor impatiently.

Federico was not to be put off. He circled the Doctor slowly as if inspecting an animal in a cage. An expression of eager cunning crept over his ugly features.

'Can you tell the future?' he asked slyly.

'I can tell *your* future,' retorted the Doctor, 'and it's likely to be very short and very unpleasant unless you listen to me.'

The Count's face darkened and he fell silent for a moment or two. Then turning to a guard he ordered Hieronymous to be summoned immediately. 'If you are making sport with us,' he snarled ominously at the Doctor, 'we shall make sport with your body. Be warned!'

Outside dusk was falling and the deep notes of the carillon rang across the city informing the inhabitants of the nightly curfew. Under the broad arch of the city gates a burly soldier was shooing the stragglers inside.

'Curfew ... curfew ... hurry along!' He prodded an overladen donkey through the opening with its equally laden master, a fat merchant from Padua. Satisfied they were the last he called out, 'Close the gates!' Above him on the ramparts the gatekeeper dodged into the winding room and the heavy doors began to close.

As the soldier was about to slip through the narrowing gap his attention was caught by a strange shrieking noise. He stopped and turned. It seemed to be coming from the air above him. He looked upwards and his whole body froze with horror. Swooping down towards him from the sky was a blinding ball of fire about ten feet in diameter. He drew his sword but it grew white hot and burst into flames. Screaming he scrabbled at the city gates trying to find the opening but they had already shut behind him. He was trapped. As he cowered against the archway the ball of fire descended upon him and engulfed his body in a blaze of dazzling light. Seconds later the light disappeared. All that remained was the hideously shrivelled form of the hapless soldier, like a piece of scarred wood struck by lightning.

Inside the palace Hieronymous was conducting his interrogation. The sorcerer weaved and bobbed around the Doctor like a monkey on a string, shooting questions at him from all sides. All the time he kept one eye cocked towards his master Federico who sat watching quietly and impassively. The astrologer's black skull cap and thick grey beard lent him a particularly sinister air in the Doctor's opinion. In addition he had noticed a suspicious looking phial of liquid which the sorcerer had brought to Federico on first entering. A look had passed between the two men suggesting complicity in some business of which the other courtiers in the room were ignorant. An uneasy fear was growing in the Doctor's mind that he had stumbled into a complicated and dangerous state of affairs. And this childish interrogation was not helping matters.

'Now answer me this,' continued the soothsayer, 'what does it signify when Venus is in opposition to Saturn and a great shadow passes over the moon?'

The Doctor sighed. 'This is really all a great waste of time.'

'Answer him!' commanded the Count, rising from his chair.

'Well it depends, doesn't it?'

'On what?' hissed Hieronymous smelling the chance of ensnaring his prey.

'On whether the cock crows three times before dawn and twelve hens lay addled eggs.'

'What school of philosophy is that?' demanded the astrologer suspiciously.

The Doctor smiled. 'I can easily instruct you. All it needs is a colourful imagination and a quick tongue.'

Hieronymous scowled blackly. 'And you, "my friend", have a mocking tongue, which can lead you into great danger.' He glanced pointedly at Federico.

The Doctor ignored this veiled threat. 'It is you who are in danger, believe me.' He turned to the Count. 'Surely you don't allow yourselves to be taken in by this clap-trap?'

'Silence!'

The Doctor shrugged his shoulders and gazed round the room. For the first time he caught sight of a new-comer, a handsome young man with long dark-brown hair standing in the shadows behind Federico's chair. He had slipped in unnoticed, and was now following the proceedings with great attention.

For the present, however, the inquisition had apparently been abandoned and Hieronymous was whispering intently into his master's ear. Seizing his opportunity the Doctor casually uncapped the phial of liquid left on the nearby table and sniffed it.

'Rat poison?' he muttered to himself, 'and in such an attractive bottle.'

'Put that down!' Federico hissed angrily.

'You shouldn't leave poison lying about,' said the Doctor, 'it's a dangerous habit.'

'Not so dangerous as your failure to answer our questions,' replied the Count coldly. He turned to the captain. 'Prepare the execution.'

The Doctor was immediately seized by half a dozen guards and dragged from the chamber.

'Now wait a minute!' he yelled, 'you haven't listened to a word I've said——' The doors of the chamber slammed shut cutting off any further protest.

Federico rose to leave but found his exit blocked by Giuliano.

'Who is that man?' asked the young Duke.

'A spy.'

'Or an alchemist?' Giuliano's questioning gaze fell on the phial of liquid.

'A draught for easing my stomach, nephew,' replied Federico and he hurriedly pocketed the phial. 'Hieronymous studies the humours of the body as well as the patterns of the stars.' He strode past Giuliano and out of the room. The young Duke looked after him thoughtfully. There was evil brewing between his uncle and Hieronymous, the signs were clear. Yet, there was little he could do except watch—and wait.

Deep beneath the city the sacrificial chamber of the Brother of Demnos reverberated to the sound of a low and eerie chanting. A file of black-cowled figures processed slowly round the bare stone altar in the middle of the chamber, intoning strange litanies and orisons. Their faces were covered by grotesque and ancient masks hideously carved out of gold and silver into fixed expressions of hate and evil. In the flickering torch-light they lent the scene a disturbing and hellish touch. As each brother passed the altar he bowed and threw a pink flower-petal onto the clean stone surface.

Then the priest entered the chamber carrying a silk cushion which he placed at one end of the altar. On it lay a gleaming sharply-pointed knife. This was the sacrificial blade.

Not far away in a cramped stone dungeon Sarah could hear the chanting. The words were foreign sounding and confused but their import was clear enough. Unless she could find a way out of this place she would end up as just another sacrifice to their wretched god, whatever his name was. She grabbed at the iron bars of the cell and tried to budge them. It was hopeless. She let out a sob of despair and sank to the floor. The utter futility of her situation was all too clear.

Then a key turned in the lock and the heavy metal door swung open. Two brothers stepped inside and swiftly seized her by the wrists while a third covered her in a long white robe. Sarah struggled as fiercely as she could, but could not prevent the robe from being put round her. Next, her head was forced back and a goblet full of liquid poured down her throat. It tasted sweet and sickly. It must have been a drug because instantly she began to feel drowsy and light-headed. Through the quickly spreading numbness she heard the voice of the priest in the doorway, soft and soothing.

'You are lucky, my child. Few have the honour of serving the great god Demnos so totally. When the moon rises over the southern obelisk your hour of glory will have come.'

The mellifluous tones grew more and more distant and Sarah realised she was losing control of her senses. She tried to fight the effects of the drug, but consciousness was ebbing faster and faster away and finally she blacked out.

In the palace the long marble corridors were deserted. The candles on the walls flickered fitfully in the evening draughts and cast long shadows across the richly patterned floors. A small door opened halfway along one of the dimly lit passages and a sinister skull-capped figure flitted into view. It was Hieronymous, the court astrologer. Swiftly and silently he traversed the corridor and disappeared down a narrow staircase.

With the speed and sureness of one who had made the journey before, he threaded his way down a maze of passageways, lower and lower until he reached the nethermost regions of the palace. Finally, he stopped in front of a rough stone wall. With practised ease he pressed his fingers against the stone-work, and the wall swung away in front of him to reveal a secret passage beyond. He stepped through, and the wall slid back into position with a clunk.

Above ground it was twilight. Normally at this hour a quiet peace would fall on the city of San Martino as all and sundry retired for the night. But now the city was alive and buzzing. In the main square in front of the palace crowds pushed and squeezed their way forward towards a raised wooden platform on which stood an executioner's block. Rows of pikemen in the scarlet and yellow livery of Count Federico stood stiffly to attention at the foot of the dais, and on all sides of the square mounted guards formed a protective cordon through which no one could escape.

The crowd grew fidgety and restless, the guards' horses snorted and pawed the ground impatiently; everyone was waiting.

Then, a line of drummers stepped forward from beneath the palace entrance and began to beat a slow and solemn roll. A gasp of fear and excitement ran through the square as the deathly figure of the executioner appeared. His chest and arms were bare and over his head he wore a black hood with eye-slits. He carried an enormous two-handed sword. At a signal from a balcony above he took up his position on the platform. In the balcony, hidden by shadows, sat Count Federico.

Suddenly, the crowd fell silent and there was no

sound apart from the measured beat of the drums. The Doctor, stern and tight-lipped, was led into the square flanked by four armed guards. At their head was the scar-faced captain who had first captured him. As the Doctor mounted the steps of the wooden platform, a ghost of a smile played around the Count's cruel mouth.

The Doctor halted in front of the block, and the drumming ended abruptly. He looked round at the sea of faces. Their expressions were curious, eager, fearful—that peculiar mixture of emotions which always accompanies moments of spectacle and violence. He raised his eyes above the crowd to the trees and hills beyond. The sky was a beautiful pale blue, fingered with red. How ironic, thought the Doctor, that he was to lose his life in this little backwater of human existence. Earth, the planet he had come to know and love as a second home, was about to dispense with his services for ever. That was, unless he could pull off the impossible—and somehow this time the odds seemed stacked too firmly against him.

He glanced about him. The platform was surrounded by pikemen and beyond them a ring of horsemen blocked any form of escape. If only he had more time to think.

'Kneel!'

He was forced to his knees by two guards who then stepped smartly away. The Doctor loosened the scarf around his neck. He was sweating. The executioner stepped forward and gently positioned his head on the block. It felt strangely comfortable.

Then, at a signal from Count Federico, the executioner raised his massive sword in a slow backwards arc and stood poised to deliver the deadly blow.

4

Sacrifice

'Excuse me,' said the Doctor lifting his head from the block. 'I always like to look my best on these occasions.' He flashed a smile at the executioner who froze like a statue in mid-swing. Carefully and unhurriedly, the Doctor began to unwind his long scarf. Then in one explosive movement he flung it round the executioner's ankles and pulled. The man tumbled onto the wooden boards in an ungainly heap, his sword narrowly missing the Doctor's head as it fell from his grasp. In the moment of confusion that followed, the Doctor leapt to his feet and took a running dive off the edge of the platform. He sailed through the air over the heads of the astonished pikemen and landed with a thud on the back of the nearest horse. With one blow he swept the rider from his saddle and dug his heels into the horse's flanks. The startled animal reared violently and bolted like a bullet from a gun.

Scattering onlookers and guards alike the Doctor hurtled towards the nearest exit from the square. Blocking his path were two pikemen and a mounted soldier but the Doctor's steed vaulted the long pointed staves like a champion hurdler and, landing expertly, wheeled round past the remaining guard who was too surprised to move.

'Fools! Stop him!' screamed Federico at the top of his voice. Tumbling over themselves in haste the remaining guards gave chase. But the Doctor had a head start and was already out of sight and racing through the cobbled streets like a man possessed. He knew it would be foolish to try and outrace his pursuers over any great distance. Ahead a low parapet ran along one side of the street. He quickly reined in the horse and jumped from the saddle. Then, giving the gallant animal a good slap on the rump, he swung over the parapet and waited, knowing the growing darkness would help protect him. Seconds later the clattering hooves of the pursuing troop thundered by inches from his head. He remained perfectly still until sure they were gone, then let out his breath and looked around. Below him was a drop of about twelve feet onto a paved terrace. Although it was growing dark, he could make out a number of paths leading from the terrace into a maze of wooden arbours and grottos. He guessed it must be part of the palace gardens. No doubt the Guard would start searching there very shortly, but at least the trees would afford him some cover. He dropped nimbly onto the terrace, and set off down a narrow winding path.

He had travelled no more than a couple of hundred yards when he heard voices calling out on either side of him. He could see the flicker of torchlight through the trees. The search parties were out quicker than he had anticipated. He hesitated, not knowing which way to turn.

Suddenly, two pikemen appeared on the pathway ahead. They let out a cry and began running towards him. In desperation the Doctor dived off the path and down a bushy slope. He slithered and stumbled to the bottom only to discover he was trapped in a dark stone grotto. Apart from the slope he had just come down there was no exit. He was walled in on all sides by what looked like ancient ruins. The excited yells of the pikemen grew nearer. He was cornered like a rat in a hole.

Then an extraordinary thing happened. As the Doctor's back pressed against the rough stonework he felt the wall behind him move! He spun round and sure enough a gap had appeared in the masonry the height of a door. He pushed against the wall with both hands, and it swung open to reveal a narrow flight of steps leading into the ground. Unable to believe his good fortune the Doctor stepped smartly through the door, and heaved it back into place behind him.

Moments later the two pikemen arrived on the other side. The Doctor could hear their astonished conversation through the wall.

'I swear he came in here,' said the first, 'and there's no way out! Are we chasing a phantom?'

'Or a worshipper of Demnos?' whispered the second, fear creeping into his voice. 'Those devils know a hundred secret ways through the city.'

'A passage? Quick then, let's find the trick!'

The Doctor held his breath as the first pikeman began to push and prod at the stonework.

'No Giovanni,' said the other restraining his companion. 'I'd not venture into those catacombs for all the gold in Rome. I know men who've tried and never been seen again!'

There was a pause and the first pikeman muttered something the Doctor did not catch. He must have been convinced by his companion's reasoning because the next thing the two of them could be heard cursing and grunting as they climbed back up the steep slope.

The Doctor breathed a sigh of relief and considered his next move. The pikeman's talk about the worshippers of Demnos had aroused his curiosity. They sounded very much like the hooded brothers who had kidnapped Sarah. If he had stumbled upon an entrance to their meeting place then he might well be able to find her. He set off cautiously down the narrow stone steps and into the thickening gloom of the catacombs.

He had not gone very far when a sixth sense alerted him to danger. A few feet ahead lay an intersection with another passage and down it he could hear footsteps approaching. He pressed himself back into a niche in the rock-wall.

The footsteps grew nearer and finally a figure in long purple robes appeared out of the darkness. It stopped at the junction of the two passageways and, facing the blank wall, stretched out its arms and pressed the stonework. From where he was hiding the Doctor could only glimpse the outline of the figure but he felt sure it was wearing a head-mask of some kind. There was a rumble and where the figure had pushed the rock-face a section of it now slid aside. The figure stepped through and the entrance closed behind him.

The Doctor waited several moments then emerged from his niche and approached the rock-face. Carefully he explored the blank wall with the tips of his fingers until he discovered a small indentation. He pressed, the same rumbling noise occurred, and the wall slid aside to reveal a further passage beyond. The Doctor tip-toed through and the secret door swung to behind him.

In a quiet ante-room in the palace Giuliano was examining the body of the sentry killed outside the city gates. A guardsman looked on, fearful and wide-eyed.

'No it is not a fire demon,' said the Prince reassuringly, 'such things are pure superstition.'

'Then what is it, sire?'

'His skin is such a strange colour. I've not seen a corpse like this before.' He frowned, genuinely puzzled, then covered the body with a sheet. 'Poor man.'

'We thought ...' mentioned the guardsman, '... with your interest in the new learning ...'

The Prince put up his hand. 'You did well to bring him to me. But the new learning does not always have answers. It means only that we must throw away old beliefs like witchcraft, sorcery and demons and trust our own intelligence.'

'I still think it could be a fine demon, sire. I once heard of a case in Florence ...'

The Prince smiled at him. 'All right. You may return to your duties.'

The guard bowed low and left the room. A moment later Marco entered.

'No further news, my lord.' He stopped as he caught sight of the body on the couch.

'He was found at the city gate, Marco.'

He lead his companion to the couch and pulled back the sheet. 'What do you make of it, old friend?'

Marco winced at the sight and he looked questioningly at his young master.

Robed in white and looking deathly pale Sarah lay unconscious on the sacrificial altar. Around her a hundred hooded figures whirled like dervishes in a mounting frenzy of religious fervour. As they danced around their victim their grotesque masks seemed to come alive in the flickering torchlight, like ghouls awakened from the dead.

The ritual continued for several minutes. Then the brothers dropped to the floor and knelt towards the altar. The High Priest appeared at one end of the chamber and made his way slowly to the head of the altar. Grasping the sacrificial blade which lay on the cushion by Sarah's head he turned and displayed it to the kneeling throng. A response of feverish excitement rang around the chamber. A second figure cloaked in purple robes and wearing a mask carved from pure gold emerged from a small hidden entrance near the altar. With its leering mouth and cruel, deep-set eyes, the masked visage seemed the embodiment of evil.

The figure approached the altar and took up a position on the highest step. The High Priest bowed to him and began to chant.

'Let the sacrifice be swift and certain lest the great god Demnos be displeased!'

'So shall it be,' replied the masked figure and taking hold of the sacrificial knife he raised it point downward over Sarah's defenceless form. The chanting of the High Priest and the responses of the brothers rose to a pitch of hysteria, echoing round the vast chamber in a cacophony of sound.

The Doctor paused. He had reached a dimly lit passage not far from the main chamber. The eerie chanting sound which he had heard for several minutes now began to ring more loudly in his ears. He hurried on, drawn by the mesmeric incantation. Intuition, sixth sense, that telepathic power which Time Lords possess told him Sarah was ahead and in danger. He rounded one more bend in the tunnel and there in front was the chamber and the source of the sound he had been following. For a second he was stunned by the sheer numbers of black hooded figures covering the floor of the cavern. But that shock was superseded by an even greater one as he spied Sarah on the altar, the sacrificial knife poised ready to plunge into her heart.

Both the High Priest and the masked figure were gazing upwards to the roof of the cavern incanting the final phrases of their votive offering. In the instant's delay, the Doctor leapt through the kneeling bodies and gained the altar steps. As the voice of the masked figure reached a climax and the knife began its rapid descent, the Doctor swept Sarah up in his arms and lifted her bodily from the path of the flashing blade. It dug into the stone surface with a steely clang almost throwing the masked figure off balance. It took a few moments for him to realise what had happened but then he let out a scream of rage and pointed to the fleeing form of the Doctor.

'Seize him!'

The High Priest ran down the altar steps followed by three brothers. The remainder were still too confused to take in the situation.

The Doctor struggled with Sarah towards the passage which led from the chamber.

The pursuing brothers were almost on him when something so remarkable occurred it halted them dead in their tracks. The entire chamber had begun to glow with an ethereal light and the sound of a great rushing wind reverberated around the cavernous walls. The brothers, including the Doctor's pursuers, turned to face the altar where the masked figure in purple now stood rooted to the spot, arms upraised in a supplicating gesture.

'Brothers, look!' he cried, 'our prayers are answered . . . our temple is restored.'

As the Doctor watched, the broken rocky masses which formed the chamber walls began to shimmer and pulsate and the ghostly outline of a beautiful, pillared temple complete in every detail filled the chamber. Then the Doctor heard a familiar whining noise and the glowing red sphere of Mandragora Energy descended through the roof of the cavern, and engulfed the altar in a dazzling blaze of light.

'What is it? What's happening?' whispered a tiny weak voice in the Doctor's ear. He turned to see Sarah, her eyes half open in an effort to regain consciousness. Thankful to be able to release her weight from his arms he lowered her carefully to the ground.

'It seems our own little bit of the Mandragora Helix has finally got here, Sarah.'

As he spoke the light around the altar faded. It was as if the stone slab had somehow absorbed the Energy.

'Time to leave,' whispered the Doctor. Taking Sarah's arm he led her on tiptoe out of the chamber.

Behind them the attention of the assembled brethren was still diverted as they gazed with awe upon their restored temple. Plucking up courage the High Priest approached the altar and bowed reverentially.

'It is a dream of two thousand years come true! How is it possible?'

'Faith, brother,' responded the masked figure, 'Faith!'

Then the High Priest let out a cry. 'Look!'

As they stared at the altar a column of radiant light appeared at one end. It was about three feet in diameter and seemed to shine straight down through the roof of the chamber.

'Stand back!' commanded the masked figure. The Priest and surrounding brethren fell away from the altar as they were bid and the masked figure slowly climbed the altar steps.

The light looked immensely dangerous, like a current of high-voltage power. The masked figure reached the top of the steps, hesitated a moment, then

since he had heard it on the lips of the pikemen it had rankled at the back of his mind.

'Have you heard of him?' asked Sarah.

The Doctor nodded. It had come in a flash of memory. 'A particularly nasty Roman cult, which was supposed to have died out in the third century.'

'So why are they still around in the fifteenth century?' Sarah's voice echoed in the darkness. 'And what have they got to do with the Mandragora Helix?'

'Put it the other way, Sarah. What has the Mandragora Helix to do with them? What we saw back there was a sub-thermal recombination of ionised plasma.'

There was a slight pause. 'Simple,' said Sarah. 'I should have thought of that.'

'The question is,' continued the Doctor, 'why a remote, obscure little planet like Earth ... what is their intention?' ... He tailed off ruminating on the problem.

'Conquest? Invasion? They want to take over Earth and fill it full of old Roman temples.'

The Doctor laughed. 'The Intelligences that inhabit the Helix don't have a physical existence in the way that you or I would understand it. They don't need Earth.'

The Doctor was about to speculate further when he received a nudge in the ribs from Sarah's elbow.

'Come in Number Seven your time is up.'

'What?'

Sarah nodded towards the darkness behind him. The Doctor whirled round. Four large shapes were advancing towards them in the gloom, their long pikes glinting in the reflected moonlight from the entrance. They surrounded the Doctor and Sarah and motioned the pair to their feet. Resistance was futile. They both obeyed and allowed themselves to be prodded out of

45

the tunnel and into the palace gardens.

'Just when the conversation was getting interesting too,' sighed the Doctor loudly and gave a wink of encouragement to Sarah.

5

The Prince Must Die

The Doctor and Sarah were led hurriedly through the gardens and into the palace itself. Once inside, their captors marched them silently along dimly lit corridors, and finally bundled them into a small wood-panelled chamber. A handsome young man with dark-brown hair and wearing fine garments rose from a table as they were thrust in. The Doctor recognised him immediately as the stranger who had observed his interrogation by Hieronymous.

The young man nodded curtly to the guards who released their hold on the prisoners and left the room.

'Whatever happened to that old-time Italian courtesy?' complained Sarah rubbing her sore wrists.

'I apologise if you were roughly handled,' said the young man. 'Speed was essential. My uncle has men searching for you everywhere.'

The Doctor looked surprised. 'Your uncle?'

The young man nodded. 'Count Federico. He has given orders that you be executed immediately you are found. Luckily, a few of the guards are still loyal to their Prince.' He gave a brief smile.

Sarah felt a sudden sense of relief. 'And that's you?'

'Giuliano, Duke of San Martino.' The young man bowed politely.

'And this is my companion, Marco.'

46

A tall fair-haired young man stepped forward from the back of the room where he had been concealed in the shadows. He bowed stiffly.

'Tell me more about your uncle,' said the Doctor.

'The Count murdered Giuliano's father,' interposed Marco with vehemence.

'Are you certain?'

Giuliano nodded. 'Certain.'

'And now he's plotting to kill Giuliano.'

'I take it you don't get on with your uncle,' smiled the Doctor.

The Prince looked serious. 'My uncle is a tyrant.'

'While Giuliano lives Federico can never claim the throne,' explained Marco.

'I do not fear so much for myself as for the people,' continued the young Prince. 'Were he ever to rule San Martino all knowledge, all attempt at learning would be suppressed.'

The Doctor nodded understandingly. 'And that's what he wants? Well Giuliano, if you don't mind my saying so you look good for at least another fifty years.'

The Prince lowered his eyes. 'I am to die. Hieronymous has predicted it.'

The Doctor gave a snort of derision. 'Hieronymous? I shouldn't take too much notice of him.'

'I try not to,' replied the Prince in a level voice. 'From the way you spoke to him I take it you are a man of science?' His eyes searched the Doctor's intelligently.

'I do dabble a little,' said the Doctor modestly.

'Excellent! I crave for contact with men of intellect and understanding.'

The Doctor seemed amused. 'How flattering! But surely you've not gone to all these lengths just to enjoy my company?'

In answer, Giuliano crossed to a screened alcove at

47

the rear of the chamber. 'There are things I want to show you, Doctor. This—for example.' He snatched back the screen to reveal a dead body on a pallet. Sarah winced. The body, once one of Federico's guards, was hideously disfigured with burn marks.

The Doctor stepped back looking grim. 'Yes Helix Energy. High ionisation. It only has to touch human tissue ...'

Giuliano looked puzzled.

'You're not talking his language, Doctor,' interjected Sarah.

'This man's body was found by the city gates,' explained the Prince. 'The guards are muttering of fire devils. I of course do not accept such superstitions.'

'Nevertheless?' enquired the Doctor.

Giuliano frowned. 'It worries me. Is it possible that something has entered the city—perhaps something conjured up by Hieronymous?'

The Doctor shook his head gravely. 'Something has certainly entered the city, Giuliano—a malevolent power quite beyond the experience of that old fake. The question is why?'

The Prince still seemed puzzled. 'I don't understand ...'

The Doctor dug his hands deep into his pockets and began pacing the room. 'Why here? Why now?'

'And what has it got to do with the Cult of Demnos?' piped up Sarah.

'Exactly,' exclaimed the Doctor. 'We seem to have rather a lot of questions. It's time we started finding a few answers.'

Outside Giuliano's chamber there were increasing signs of activity. The clank of armour and shuffling footsteps echoed along the palace corridors indicating

48

the search was being intensified, and through the open window came distant yells of guards still hunting the gardens.

Meanwhile Count Federico strode about his chamber like a caged tiger, awaiting news. There was a knock at his door and the scar-faced captain entered and bowed.

'Well?' snarled the Count impatiently. 'Have you nothing to report?'

'Only that they have disappeared, sire.'

'Impossible!' exploded Federico. He aimed a kick at a nearby footstool.

'There has been no sign of them since they were last seen in the palace gardens.'

The Count's face grew black with fury. 'They must be found! Something about that Doctor disturbs me greatly. I want every corner of the palace searched. Take all the men you need.' He turned his back on the captain and waved him angrily out of the room.

The captain bowed silently but remained where he stood. 'Sire,' he said softly.

Federico's broad back remained firmly turned. 'What is it?'

The captain took out a piece of paper from his belt. 'This list—it was prepared by the Duke Giuliano's secretary.'

Federico span round and snatched the list. 'To the King of Naples?' he read aloud, '... the Duke of Milan ... the Duke of Padua ... the Doge of Venice ... Signoria of Florence ...' His expression grew more enraged by each name.

'They are the rulers who have accepted Giuliano's invitation and are coming to San Martino,' explained the captain in a servile tone.

A look of contempt appeared on the Count's ugly face. 'To celebrate his accession to the Dukedom. The arrogant puppy!' He screwed up the list in his hand, hurled it against the wall and stormed out of the chamber.

Moments later there was a sharp rat-a-tat at Hieronymous's door and Federico strode in. Hieronymous looked up in surprise from a pile of ancient charts he was studying.

'I did not say enter,' he said curtly. His face wore a cool and reserved expression unlike his normal obsequious manner.

'What?' Federico seemed momentarily taken aback.

'I wish to be left alone,' snapped the old soothsayer and returned to his charts.

'In this palace, astrologer, I come and go as I please,' growled Federico.

'This is my private room.'

The Count's eyes narrowed and he leant forward threateningly. 'Whatever room you have here is because I allow it. I've warned you before, Hieronymous, do not get above yourself.'

Hieronymous said nothing for a moment then responded in a more conciliatory fashion. 'I have studying to do. But if there is something urgent you want?'

'Yes, it is urgent!' shouted Federico, then realising he might be overheard lowered his voice. 'We cannot wait until Mars or Saturn or whatever other nonsense it was you said—Giuliano must die at once.' He fixed Hieronymous with a penetrating stare.

'It is not nonsense,' retorted the astrologer.

Federico continued unheeding. 'He's called a gathering here of all the leading scholars and philosophers in Italy and their patrons.'

Hieronymous looked up sharply. 'Gathering?'

Federico nodded impatiently. 'Don't you see what

50

it means? With all those important people here, at his invitation, he will establish his power in the state for good.'

'So?'

Federico banged his fist down on Hieronymous's charts. 'So it will be harder to get rid of him!' He paused for breath. 'He must die. Tonight!'

Hieronymous drew himself up to his full height and shook his head solemnly. 'It cannot be.'

'Why not? I have the poison.' Federico scowled. 'I want you to announce that you have made a new finding,' he waved his arm airily, 'some new conjunction has come to light. You'll think of something.' He pressed his face close to Hieronymous. 'Sudden death!'

Hieronymous withdrew. 'You're asking me to invent a horoscope.'

'That's what you always do,' snapped the Count.

A look of hurt appeared on the soothsayer's visage. 'Do you know what it is you are mocking?' He raised his voice. 'Do you know what power is held by the celestial bodies? They are not at our beck and call.'

Federico took hold of Hieronymous by the shoulders and shook him violently. 'I'm asking you to help me, as you did before.' His voice grew menacing. 'Giuliano must die tonight! Do you understand?' He bellowed in the soothsayer's ears, 'Tonight!'

6

The Secret of the Temple

'Spirit from the heavens? I thought you were a man of science, Doctor.'

The speaker was Giuliano and his handsome features wore a vexed expression. He was now alone with the Doctor and Sarah having dispatched Marco to keep unwelcome visitors at bay.

The Doctor, who had been pacing up and down all this time expounding theories, suddenly stopped and smiled.

'It's rather hard to explain the concept of Helix energy—either sub- or super-thermal ionisation—in a medieval vocabulary.'

'I think you're doing a great job,' interposed Sarah, picking at a bunch of grapes on the table in front of her. 'But you haven't explained why these spirits are appearing in romantic old fifteenth-century Italy, have you?' She popped a grape in her mouth.

'Perhaps because the worshippers of Demnos offer a ready made power-base,' replied the Doctor suddenly attracted by the idea. 'And what better time than the fifteenth century? The time between the dark ages of superstition and the dawn of Reason.'

Sarah frowned. 'You mean if they can gain control of Earth now . . . through an ancient religion . . .?'

'That could be the plan.' The Doctor turned excitedly to the young Prince. 'Giuliano, that temple must be destroyed!'

'But only ruins stand there now, Doctor.'

'Those ruins are a focal point for enormous forces,' exclaimed the Doctor. 'The Helix Energy has penetrated every stone.' He moved towards the door. 'Is there a way I can get to the temple without being seen?'

Guiliano nodded, impressed by the Doctor's conviction and sense of urgency. 'I'll show you myself.'

'No. It's better if I go alone.'

The Prince shook his head. 'It's too dangerous.'

The Doctor hesitated, looked at Sarah. They could not risk being caught again.

'All right,' he said. 'As far as the temple, but no further.'

Giuliano crossed to a large wooden chest and took out a couple of swords.

'Here!' He threw one to the Doctor who caught it expertly, and executed a series of clever flourishes.

'If I'd known we were coming I'd have practised my épée,' he exclaimed with a twinkle in his eye. Sarah grinned.

'We'll take the back staircase,' explained Giuliano. He opened the door warily and, satisfied that none of Federico's guards were lurking in the shadows, led them quickly away.

Moments later the three of them emerged from a rear door of the palace, crossed a series of small cobbled courtyards, and disappeared into the welcoming cover of the gardens.

It was nearly dawn. A slight dew lay on the grass dampening their clothes as they brushed through. The young Prince led them down a maze of hidden pathways until the palace was left far behind. There was no sign of search parties and they made rapid progress. At one point the Doctor thought they passed the secret entrance he had discovered earlier, but Giuliano did not pause. The gardens lacked any reliable landmarks and various paths and grottoes were deceptively similar.

After about twenty minutes the track grew steep and rocky then suddenly dropped down beside a small stream. On the far side a woody bluff rose up a hundred feet or so, its side covered with bushes and thick overhanging trees. Giuliano guided them on stepping stones across the stream, and up to the face of the rocky mount.

Scattered about the foot were large lumps of masonry, ancient broken pillars of Greek or Roman design. They had been there for centuries probably, covered with thick moss and trailing vines.

'This is it,' said Giuliano. He pulled back one of the bushes to reveal a hidden entrance running into the hillside.

The Doctor peered into the forbidding gloom, then turned and addressed the other two. 'From this point on I must go alone.'

Giuliano was about to protest but Sarah held his arm and shook her head. This was a matter for the Doctor. She had come to recognise times when it was best not to interfere—when the Doctor seemed guided by inner forces not fully understandable to humans. This was one of those occasions.

The Doctor gripped his sword firmly and without a further word disappeared into the dark tunnel.

From a hidden cache on the other side of the stream a helmeted figure watched quietly as Sarah and Giuliano retreated to the cover of a ruined column. He was dressed in the scarlet and yellow livery of Federico's bodyguard. He waited a few moments until satisfied they were not going to leave, then slipped away furtively through the trees in the direction of the palace.

Federico was prowling his chamber like a fretful insomniac when there was a perfunctory knock at the door and the captain burst in, breathless.

'Sire, they've been seen. They're with the Duke Giuliano at the ruined temple.'

Federico's tired eyes opened wide with surprise. 'The Duke is with them? Are you certain?'

The captain nodded vehemently. 'Otherwise the

men would have seized them at once.'

Federico ceased his prowling and an evil smile flickered across his saturnine features. 'The ruined temple, you say?'

'In that direction.'

The Count weighed this information carefully. The outlines of a devious stratagem began to formulate in his head.

'Excellent, excellent,' he whispered at last. 'A chance to solve all my problems in one blow.'

The captain nervously fingered the scar on his cheek, unsure of his master's meaning.

'It will appear like a sacrifice,' continued the Count, relishing the scenario in his mind's eye. 'A human sacrifice to the gods. Our hands will be guiltless.' He hugged himself with delight at the prospect.

Admiration and awe dawned on the captain's face as he grasped the drift of Federico's plan. 'A sacrifice ... yes ... the evil pagans who worship Demnos ...'

'Get your men quickly!' commanded Federico and he snapped his fingers for a valet to bring his cloak. 'I will lead them myself.'

The Doctor felt his way carefully along the darkened tunnel. There was no torchlight here, unlike the other parts of the catacombs and in ten minutes he had travelled no further than a hundred yards.

After a while he began to notice a change in the air around him. A faint draught brushed his face. That meant there must be a large opening ahead. He quickened his pace. As he did so the walls of the tunnel became more distinct. A source of light lay somewhere in front.

Abruptly the tunnel grew wider and turning a corner the Doctor found himself staring into the sacrificial chamber. He realised he had come out on the far side, exactly facing the exit from which he had made his escape earlier with Sarah.

He scanned the chamber carefully for any activity. It was empty, save for the ever-flickering torches in their metal sockets on the walls.

In the centre of the ruined cavern stood the sacrificial altar grey and bare.

The Doctor picked his way stealthily across the rock-strewn floor and approached the altar. As he did so a sudden cracking noise rang out behind him. He froze.

Silence.

For several seconds he remained still as a statue, inwardly coiled like a taut spring ready for action.

But there was no further sound. He turned and surveyed the cavern once more. The torchlight threw curious dancing shadows on the walls, grotesque shapes which appeared and disappeared like phantoms; otherwise the chamber was empty of life.

He continued towards the altar. Then, as he reached the lowest step, the noise occurred again— much louder this time. It sounded like stone walls shifting and crumbling. Simultaneously the chamber was illuminated by an eerie glow which burned the Doctor's eyes. He was filled with an unaccountable urge to escape, but as he ran towards the tunnel exit a large wall materialised in front of him with a deafening crash. Blindly he stumbled towards the other side of the cavern and a second wall blocked his path. The ghostly Temple of Demnos had sprung up before his very eyes! Panic-stricken he turned this way and that seeking escape but all around him thick stone walls seemed to be hemming him in. He was trapped.

Then another, different noise assailed his ears. It was the high-pitched wail of Mandragora Energy. It seemed to be rushing and shrieking in diminishing circles above his head. In an explosion of sound, he felt it penetrate his skull. His brain was pierced by an agonising noise which grew louder and louder. The shrill note seemed to plumb the very depths of his being. The Doctor felt he was spinning out of control in a vertiginous whirlpool of sound. He sank to his knees, his face contorted with indescribable pain. At the same time a distant booming laughter rolled around the cavernous temple, as if in mockery at his helpless agony.

Outside the entrance to the catacombs Giuliano and Sarah sat waiting on one of the upturned columns. Sarah felt nervous and anxious but tried not to show it. She was impressed by the young Duke's quiet confidence and did not wish to reveal how desperate she thought their situation really was. As Giuliano spoke in his soft firm voice, she also realised she found him very attractive. The fact that five hundred years of history lay between them and not just a few feet of grass only heightened the peculiar fascination the young Prince was beginning to exert on her. She listened earnestly as he explained about his studies.

'You see, I have a theory that the world is really a sphere,' he said solemnly.

Sarah smiled. 'I don't think that idea will ever catch on.'

'Why not?' exclaimed Giuliano. 'Other scientists are coming to the same conclusion—that the Earth cannot possibly be flat because ...'

Sarah suddenly grabbed his arm. 'What was that?' she whispered.

'Nothing ... You see it's really obvious when you think about it. It's ...' He broke off suddenly, and drew his sword. Sarah followed his gaze. On all sides the bushes were parting to reveal Federico's soldiers advancing on them, swords at the ready.

'Quick, the Doctor!' cried Giuliano and gave Sarah a shove.

As she raced for the hidden entrance Giulano leapt over the broken pillar and positioned himself with his back to an over-hanging rock. At the same moment, a voice rang out from across the stream.

'Kill him!'

Giuliano just caught sight of his uncle's menacing shape, then the soldiers were upon him in a flurry of clashing steel.

Sarah reached the entrance to the catacombs and dived in. The sudden blackness was so unexpected she stopped in her tracks for several seconds. Then, calling the Doctor's name as loud as she could, she stumbled on through the empty darkness.

'Doctor! Doctor!'

The sound echoed dully along the winding tunnel as she blundered along, moaning and panting with exertion.

All at once something moved in the gloom ahead. She ran forward, tripping over the path.

'Doctor!'

A hand seized her round the throat. She screamed with fright and started to struggle. But more hands pinioned her arms and legs with a vice-like grip. Then a ghostly voice inches from her ear whispered in the blackness.

'Demnos will not be cheated of his pleasure this time, little one.'

Sarah's blood ran cold as she recognised the macabre tones of the High Priest.

7

The Spell of Evil

The Doctor stirred, consciousness seeped back into his body. His muscles were rigid with tension, his face grey like the cold stone floor on which he lay. He lifted his head and waves of nausea immediately flooded his nervous system. He felt drained of all energy, all will-power. It was as if Mandragora had shown him, with one flick of its little finger, how weak and puny he really was.

He clambered to his feet, fought the spinning vertigo which still clutched him in its grasp. A thousand sledge hammers crashed inside his head, the cavern walls floated drunkenly before his eyes.

As he stood there swaying unsteadily from side to side a faint cry penetrated the pounding in his skull. It sounded familiar yet he could not formulate its meaning.

He heard it again, a distant desperate cry, and this time he recognised it. His own name. Someone was calling for him. Hazily he peered about him. Flickering torchlight on looming craggy walls. A solitary stone altar. On the ground nearby a bare sword.

With a sudden surge his brain clicked into gear and he remembered. The cries had ceased. He hurriedly snatched up the sword and scrambled towards the exit.

Outside the catacombs Giuliano was fighting for his life. But because he was still the Prince, his attackers lacked the will to press home their advantage. Shielded at his back by the rock-face, Giuliano was containing their challenge.

'So, Uncle,' he cried. 'You need an army to do your work!' He felled a guard with an expert thrust.

From across the stream Federico hurled orders and abuse at his men.

'On, you craven-gutted curs, he is but one man!'

Suddenly the soldiers on Giuliano's right flank began to fall back as a second swordsman engaged them from the rear.

'You can't count, Count!' exclaimed a familar voice and the tall figure of the Doctor, sword in hand, appeared. Surprised by this unexpected and vigorous assault Federico's men momentarily scattered.

'Take the sorcerer, too!' commanded Federico. 'A gold piece to the first that splits him!'

Spurred on by their master's threats the soldiers renewed their attack. One, a large vicious-looking fellow, worked his way around the back of the Doctor and raised his sword for the kill.

'Behind you, Doctor!' warned Giuliano.

In one movement the Doctor did a neat side-step, disarmed the soldier with a blow to the wrist, and sent him sprawling into the group around Giuliano. The diversion enabled the young Prince to gain the Doctor's side.

'Thanks—this way!' shouted the Doctor.

Blades flashing, the two of them retreated through the ruins, their attackers milling round them like wolves. Suddenly Giuliano dropped his sword and fell with a cry of pain. He had received a savage jab to the right shoulder.

Federico gave a yell of triumph. 'Death to Giuliano! Now!—Now!'

But the Doctor stood his ground over the wounded Prince and met the onslaught head on. With lightning speed and accuracy he dispatched the two leading assailants. Then, parrying the thrusts of a third, he planted a foot firmly on the the man's breast-plate and sent him hurtling down at the feet of the advancing wave.

'I assure you this is hurting you more than me,' he announced calmly as his attackers picked themselves up in disarray.

In the momentary pause the Doctor gathered his strength for what was going to be the final, deadly rush. As he stood back panting from his exertion a sudden horde of black-hooded figures poured out of the hillside like ants from a nest.

'The brethren!' howled Federico in dismay.

As he watched the black throng swarmed over his guards sending them staggering and reeling in every direction. So swift and unexpected was the attack that Federico's men had no time to regroup. Although the brethren were armed with no more than wooden staves and knives their numbers overwhelmed the armed soldiers who began to retreat in confusion.

'To me! To me! Back to the palace!' Federico rallied his men, his face dark as thunder. The guards tumbled into the stream knocking into each other in the confusion. On the far bank the scar-faced captain waited, cursing and hitting them as they emerged soaked and bedraggled from the water. In the mêlée the Doctor managed to drag Giuliano to his feet and together they slipped away unseen to the catacomb entrance. Why the brethren had chosen to aid them in their struggle against Federico puzzled the Doctor. Still, he had little time to ponder their lucky escape.

As they entered the mouth of the tunnel they heard the sound of running feet ahead. The Doctor just had time to press himself and Giuliano into a crevice in the wall before a dozen brethren rushed past. The Doctor felt their rough woollen cloaks brush his face

61

as they swept by, but the darkness and the haste of the brethren saved them from discovery.

'That was fortunate!' whispered the Doctor. He helped Giuliano out of the crevice. 'What happened to Sarah?'

'She came down here for you, Doctor.' The Prince stared hard into the gloom. 'You mean you have not seen her?'

The Doctor shook his head. 'She must still be wandering about the catacombs. Come on.'

He started to move off but stopped as Giuliano let out a moan and sank to the ground.

'You'd better let me look at that arm,' said the Doctor gently. He had overlooked the extent of Giuliano's injury. He ripped off the blood-soaked shirt sleeve and inspected the wound as best he could in the dim light. The point of the sword had penetrated just below the shoulder-blade. Luckily it was a flesh wound, and nothing important had been severed. Expertly the Doctor began to bind up the cut using the torn shirt. Giuliano's face, pale and drawn, tried to hide his pain.

'You've not spent all your time in books, Doctor,' he said gratefully. 'I owe you my life.'

The Doctor concentrated on binding the wound. 'Finest swordsman I ever saw was a captain—this should staunch the bleeding—in Cleopatra's bodyguard.' He wound the material tightly and started to knot it. 'He was kind enough to hand out a few points. Keep still.'

Giuliano winced as the tourniquet was pulled taut. 'Did you get to the temple, Doctor?'

'Yes. The Mandragora Helix is there all right. It's up to some nasty tricks. There we are.' He stepped back and admired his handiwork. 'Florence Nightingale would be very pleased with that little lash up.' He smiled encouragingly at the Prince.

Giuliano looked puzzled by the strange reference but nodded. The wound certainly felt easier.

'Come on then. I must find out what's happened to Sarah.' The Doctor lifted him to his feet and together they set off slowly through the chilly darkness.

The High Priest led Sarah and her guards along a maze of rock strewn tunnels, a flaring brand held high above his head. Here and there trickles of water ran down the walls to form rivulets beneath their feet and several times Sarah caught sight of giant bats hanging upside down in huddles. Apart from the High Priest her captors were once again masked, their grotesque features leering at her like ghouls from hell as they continued their journey. There was something so inexpressibly evil about those faces, something non-human—it made her blood run cold. She knew in her bones there would be no question of reasoning with these people. They were fanatics, maniacs, impervious to sympathy. She had been lucky to escape their clutches once. They would make certain it did not happen again.

Abruptly the High Priest stopped. The tunnel had reached a dead end, a blank wall. The High Priest pressed his right hand against one of the stones and the wall fell mysteriously away before them to reveal a large ante-chamber beyond.

Sarah was prodded in and she heard the stone wall grind shut behind them. Facing her as she entered, expecting her, stood a tall and sinister figure, his head encased in a gruesome mask carved from pure gold. The nose was flat and cruel, the cheeks furrowed with deep lines of torment, the eyes blank slits shadowing the real eyes behind. His body was cloaked in rich purple robes surmounted by a peaked hood in the same colour.

Sarah eyed this awesome apparition in fear and bewilderment. Her heart skipped a beat. Even though she had been drugged, she knew instantly that this was the masked figure who had officiated at the sacrificial ceremony.

The High Priest pushed Sarah forward. 'It is an omen. The Mighty Demnos delivered his victim to us. She is the chosen sacrifice.'

The masked figure stepped up to Sarah and examined her closely. 'This one assists the foreign sorcerer. She may yet assist him to his death before her hour of glory.'

The High Priest seemed taken aback. 'But Master, the great blade of our god thirsts for blood ...'

'Patience,' replied the masked figure. 'Before the night ends, priest, there will be blood in plenty. That I promise.' His commanding tones silenced his acolyte who lowered his head in obeisance.

'We of the brethren bow to your command, Master.'

'Then bind her well so that she may not struggle or cry out—and bring her to my chamber.'

Before she could protest Sarah was roughly seized. A gag was forced into her mouth and thick ropes were produced from a cell in the corner to bind her wrists and arms. Then the High Priest touched a secret mechanism in the wall, and once more she was bundled out into the forbidding, subterranean world of the brethren.

Sweating and breathless, Count Federico sat sprawled in a red velvet armchair in his palace rooms. His face wore a disgruntled frown as a white-haired retainer dabbed his brow with a large silk handkerchief.

Through the open casement a loud fanfare sounded from the direction of the city gates. At the same time there was a knock at the door and the scar-faced captain strode in looking anxious.

'The Duke of Milan is arriving, sire.'

Federico scowled at this unwelcome piece of news. 'Get this muck out of here!' he snapped at the servant. 'Bring me clean linen. Hurry! You oaf!'

The servant scuttled out. Federico crossed to the window and stared angrily across the rooftops. 'And that fox-faced old blowhard, the Doge, will be here within the hour. His advance riders are carousing in the taverns even now.' He turned and glared at the captain.

The captain shuffled his feet. 'What's to be done, sire? They must be greeted.'

'That fat clown of a chancellor must meet them,' thundered Federico. 'Say I have been stricken with an ague. Before night comes, Rossini, you and I have work to do!' He bore down on the captain jabbing the man's breastplate to emphasise the point.

'I have a score of men searching for the Prince. He has not returned to the palace.'

'Then we must search the city. He's skulking in some stinking hovel.' Federico thrust his face inches from Rossini's. 'I've gone too far to stop now. I must see Giuliano's liver fed to the dogs by sunrise!' His eyes glinted evilly as he spat the words in the captain's face. Rossini remained perfectly still, not flinching. He had experienced his master's wrath before.

'But the deed must be stealthy, sire,' he ventured after a moment. 'With so many visitors of rank lodged in San Martino ...'

'Peasant!' exploded Federico. 'Do I need your pig-brained counsel?' He struck the captain a fierce blow across the cheek.

65

'Sire.'

'Listen, Rossini, Giuliano is a traitor! The prince of a Christian state mixing with the followers of Demnos. Taking part in their filthy black rites. You and I are witness of this!' His voice reached a crescendo. 'Oh no, I have him now!' He clenched the palm of his hand in satisfaction: 'I have him here! The Holy Father himself will kiss my hand for cleansing the state of San Martino.' He touched his knuckles to his lips and leered malevolently at Rossini out of the corner of one eye.

The Doctor and Giuliano threaded their way slowly through the dark twisting tunnels. Every so often they were forced to stop and hide as members of the brethren flitted back and forth like shadows. They seemed to be posted at all the entrances to the sacrificial chamber and the Doctor was obliged to pursue a circuitous route which grew more and more confusing at each intersection.

Somewhere, somehow they had taken a wrong turning. He had never been in such a maze—a rabbit warren of fetid, foul-smelling corridors. He felt baffled, impotent—a prisoner in some kind of hell. He realised he must be tired, having gone without sleep for several days now. The thought of finding Sarah was growing more and more remote and yet the Doctor knew he must keep on searching. Wherever she was and whatever had befallen her it was his responsibility and only he was capable of doing anything about it. He strengthened his grip on the wounded Prince and lengthened his stride.

For what seemed an eternity Sarah was half pushed,

half dragged along an endless labyrinth of dark stone corridors. Cold, bruised, and utterly exhausted she at last fell into a semi-conscious haze, her body numbed by the tightness of her bonds. At one point she thought the ground began to slope upwards, but that could just have been the effects of tiredness. She remembered climbing a flight of steps, and being led into a warmer, closer atmosphere, heavy with a cloying sickly smell. Then she must have lost consciousness because when she came round she was lying on a rough pallet in the corner of a room. She was still bound and gagged.

A thick woollen curtain divided where she was lying from the rest of the room. She could hear voices muttering beyond it, but could not make out what they were saying.

'Why did you call on our brethren to save the young Prince, Master?'

The speaker was the High Priest. He addressed Hieronymous in a low voice at the far end of the astrologer's chamber. The old soothsayer had removed his cloak and mask and was now busy adding herbs and powders to a bubbling pot.

'His life has yet some value,' he replied quietly.

'But he is no more in the eye of Demnos than any other unbeliever.' Hieronymous ceased stirring his concoction and fixed the High Priest with a curious piercing stare. 'Giuliano's appointment with death is already written. Not Count Federico, nor any other mortal must anticipate the mighty Demnos.'

The High Priest nodded obediently. 'Even so, I fear the Count will now bring all his soldiers to bear against us.'

Hieronymous raised his arms heavenwards in a ritual gesture.

'Faith, Brothers! You have seen the sign of Demnos.' His dark eyes burned in their sockets with manic fervour.

'The miracle as written in the prophecies,' incanted the Priest in reply.

'Then let the word be spread through the city— guard the sacred temple. The great god's dwelling-place must not be defiled by unbelievers in the last few hours. Now go! Hurry!' He pointed commandingly to the door. The High Priest bowed low and left without further word.

Hieronymous returned to his brew. He ladled a measure from the pot, added water and sniffed the result carefully. Apparently satisfied, he poured the mixture into a glass and set it down gently on the table.

Then, crossing to the alcove, he snatched back the woollen curtain and stood gazing at the bound and gagged form on the pallet.

Sarah viewed his abrupt appearance with a mixture of alarm and curiosity. She had never seen this bearded oddly clothed figure before and yet there was something familiar about him. She wondered whether it might be the infamous Hieronymous the Doctor had mentioned, the old fraud himself. Now she could glimpse the rest of the room it certainly resembled a den of astromancy and magic.

The figure knelt beside her and gently released the gag from her mouth. Then he untied the ropes around her wrists. Sarah stretched her neck and arms with grateful relief. She was free to move but weak enough to fall.

The stranger had crossed to a table and now returned holding a glass full of a brightly coloured liquid. He placed it to her lips.

'Do not resist, my child.' His voice was silky, soothing and not unfamiliar.

Sarah felt the fumes from the potion rising in her nostrils, pungent like a heady spice. It made her cough violently and struggle for breath.

'The aroma is sweet,' whispered the leering stranger. Holding her head he began to force the mixture down her throat. His grip was gentle but insistent. Weakened by her ordeal Sarah could not prevent herself from swallowing one or two drops.

Immediately a dizzy intoxicating sensation spread through her body, her head grew thick and muzzy. The room grew misty and swayed around her.

Then her attention was caught by something bright and shiny a few inches from her face, a crystal pendant. It began to swing slowly and rhythmically before her eyes. Somewhere in the distance she could hear the voice.

'Now child—whom do you serve?'

It sounded warm and friendly as if Sarah had known it all her life. She felt a surge of trust and affection towards its soft mellifluous tones.

'I serve you,' she heard herself say.

'And the Doctor?'

Sarah paused. A preposterous thought had formed in her head; something she had known all along, something which was blindingly obvious. What a fool she had been not to see it before. His strange manner, his alien powers, his magical possessions.

'The Doctor is a sorcerer.'

'And? . . .'

The dark face smiled from behind the spinning crystal.

'The Doctor is evil.'

'And?'

Sarah struggled for inspiration. This friendly smiling voice was good. The Doctor was its enemy. Therefore the Doctor was evil.

'And must be destroyed.'

Sarah gasped as she said the words. The crystal spun faster and faster, a mesmerising ball of light burning its image into Sarah's brain, blotting out all other sensations except that seductive insinuating voice.

'All this you will forget. All but your purpose.'

Sarah nodded. The crystal suddenly disappeared and instead she felt her hand caressed by a cold metal object, long and pointed.

'When you stand close, and the Doctor suspects nothing, you will strike him down,' commanded the voice. 'One scratch will be sufficient.'

Through blurred vision Sarah looked at her hand. In it lay a gleaming steel bodkin about four inches long with an ornamental head.

'The hand of a friend is a subtle but certain weapon.' The stranger took the bodkin and pinned it gently onto the front of Sarah's dress like a brooch.

'Now you must be returned to the Doctor's side. How glad he will be to see his young companion. And when I command you must kill him.'

He led Sarah to a concealed flight of steps behind a curtain. Then, gazing deeply into her eyes one more time, he commanded her to go. Hypnotised and spellbound, Sarah nodded meekly and descended the staircase. Her mission, to kill the Doctor!

8

Torture!

'Well?'

The challenge, delivered with rasping menace, hung in the air like an executioner's blade above Rossini's head.

70

The captain stared miserably at the patterned floor of Federico's chamber. 'Nothing, sire.' He blurted the words out fearfully.

Federico's eyes narrowed and his face swelled with fury.

'You inept clod! What were my orders?'

'We have searched everywhere.'

Federico rose from his chair and advanced on the captain, his riding crop raised threateningly.

'Dunghead!'

He brought the crop across the captain's cheek, leaving a vicious red weal where it struck. The captain flinched but stood his ground.

'Fail me, Rossini, and I'll swear you'll breakfast on burning coals! I want the Duke's head here—tonight!' He cracked the whip across a table sending objects flying in all directions. 'I want to spit in his sightless eyeballs!'

The captain eyed the whip and measured his words carefully. 'Sire, we can only think he has taken to the catacombs.'

'The catacombs!'

'A hundred men might search those galleries for a month, sire, and still find nothing. They say there are places where the bat droppings are twice the height of a man.'

'They say, they say!' the Count hissed contemptuously. 'The truth of it, Rossini, is you've no stomach for the task.'

'If it is your wish, my lord, I'll take the entire guard and begin the search this very night.'

Federico grunted and paced the floor thoughtfully. 'No . . . no, it's true. If he's gone into that warren he'll be harder to find than a louse in a beggar's rags . . .' He paused. 'But sometime he'll have to come out again—

or die like a sewer rat.' He wagged a finger knowingly at Rossini.

The captain permitted himself a smile. 'And when he does we will be ready for him.'

'Of course you will, numskull! But more than that.' Federico chuckled malevolently. 'We are going to prove that the Duke Giuliano has been a secret devotee of the cult of Demnos!'

The young Prince was still breathing uneasily and the pain had returned. The Doctor paused for a moment to give him respite. As they rested in the un-healthy darkness they could hear the bats squeaking and dodging about their heads.

'Doctor, there is a stench of evil in these catacombs,' gasped Giuliano.

The Doctor sounded surprised. 'Don't tell me you're afraid?'

'Of course not.' The Prince's voice was clear and firm.

'Come on then!' The Doctor started to lift Giul-iano to his feet. As he did so there was a sudden grind-ing noise and part of the stonework behind them began to move.

'Doctor!' whispered Giuliano.

Slowly a large mass of rock swung aside to reveal a secret entrance. The Doctor guessed he must have triggered the mechanism while levering Giuliano to his feet. He grinned. 'The ancients who built this place knew a thing or two.'

He stepped through the secret opening. Giuliano did likewise. Immediately the massive rock swung to behind them. Ahead lay a curving corridor lit at in-tervals by burning torches set into the walls.

The Doctor suddenly realised it was the door

through which he had first followed the masked figure; only this time they were passing through it in the opposite direction. In that case they were heading towards the palace!

Suddenly there was a sound, like a low moan.

'Was that you, Giuliano?'

'No.'

The Doctor drew his sword and advanced carefully into the shadows. Twenty paces on there was a bend in the tunnel and the torchlight seemed brighter. The Doctor turned the corner and let out a gasp of surprise. There lying limply against the stonework was the prostrate form of Sarah Jane.

'Sarah!'

The Doctor darted forward and knelt over her. Behind him Giuliano scrambled to his feet and ran to join him.

'Is she all right?'

'I think so.' The Doctor gently shook her shoulder, 'Sarah ... Sarah.'

Slowly her eyes opened and looked dazedly around. 'Where ... where am I?' She tried to sit up. The Doctor put his arm round her comfortingly.

'Her eyes are strange,' remarked Giuliano.

The Doctor nodded. 'What happened, Sarah?'

'The brothers ... two of them ... I ... I can't remember much.'

Giuliano frowned. 'Why would they leave her here?'

'Perhaps they were planning to come back for her,' speculated the Doctor. He looked around. 'This passage runs under the palace.'

'How do you know?' Giuliano sounded surprised.

'The first time I saw him the leader of the cult, the masked figure, was coming this way. He probably uses it regularly.' The Doctor's clear blue eyes fixed the young Prince with a penetrating stare.

'I don't think the Mandragora Intelligences hijacked the TARDIS and sent us to this point of space and time without reason. There is already somebody here sensitive to its influence. Probably there has been some kind of tenuous link for centuries.'

Giuliano realised the Doctor was referring to the brethren and their leader and the thought of that superstitious band possessing genuine powers filled him with foreboding.

'Doctor, give me a hand.' Sarah's pert voice cut through the air. She seemed to have suddenly recovered.

'Are you fit to move?' asked the Doctor.

'I think so.'

He helped her gently to her feet. 'Come on then. Solvitur ambulando.'

'What?'

'Latin,' explained Giuliano. 'The question is solved by walking.'

'Oh,' said Sarah. 'Thanks. Hey! Never mind Latin. I don't even speak Italian. Doctor, how is it I can understand Giuliano? I've never thought of that before?'

The Doctor turned and gave her a curious look. 'Don't worry about it, Sarah. I'll try to explain later.' He led them off down the corridor and his face betrayed a sign of anger.

Marco waited anxiously in Giuliano's room toying with the telescope on the table. His master and the two strange visitors had been missing for hours and he was beginning to grow anxious. Luckily no one had enquired too closely into the Prince's whereabouts but sooner or later he would have to think of an explanation. There had been unusual activity too about the palace. He had seen several troops of Federico's guards leave and then return apparently from some skirmish outside the city.

Marco inwardly recoiled at Federico's name. For years he had nursed a growing fear of the Count's evil ambitions. More than once he had had to interpose on Giuliano's behalf when Federico's poisonous lies had threatened to turn the old Duke against his son. Now, with the old man gone, Federico's wolfish craving for the throne seemed to know no bounds.

But whatever events the future might bring, Marco felt strong and proud in his loyalty to the Prince.

As he gazed out of the window, his mind full of these thoughts, a thunderous knocking on the door brought him to his senses.

'Open! Open! In the name of Duke Giuliano.'

Marco hurriedly crossed to the door as the knocking was repeated. Thank goodness some of the guards were still loyal to the Prince. He unbolted the door.

Immediately, a squad of pikemen rushed into the room headed by Rossini. Marco realised too late that these were not Giuliano's men but Federico's. He drew his sword to put up a fight but was quickly overpowered and dragged kicking out of the room.

The Doctor paused and beckoned to Giuliano.

'Anywhere you know?'

The passage had broadened out and here and there red brickwork showed through the walls. There was also a faint musty smell as if casks of wine had once been stored nearby.

Giuliano's face broke into a grin.

'We're in the palace dungeons. I remember my father once spoke of a secret passage——'

75

The Doctor nodded. 'Excellent. Do you think you can find it?'

Giuliano advanced cautiously into the shadows ahead.

'Yes. Here it is,' he whispered. He pointed to what looked like a small alcove in the wall, but when the Doctor and Sarah got nearer they could see it was a narrow flight of steps winding upwards in a spiral.

'Right. Follow me,' said the Doctor. 'And quietly now.' He started up the steps, sword in hand.

Hieronymous was seated in Federico's room, alone. He had requested an audience and was now waiting for the Count to appear. The stars had revealed an unhappy conjunction, the signs were clearly there, he would not be doing his duty to keep such warnings from his Lordship. Even so Hieronymous now had much weightier problems on his mind, and as he sat awaiting the Count his thoughts began to wander. The events of the last twenty-four hours had thrown his entire being into a state of feverish tumult. That he, Hieronymous, son of a poor peasant from Bologna should become the chosen vessel of powers beyond the dreams of men! Not only San Martino and all of the Italian states, but the very world itself might be within his grasp. What could he not achieve then? What pleasures, what powers could be denied him? His lips quivered as scenes of undisguised degeneracy passed through his mind's eye.

But for the moment he must bide his time, listen carefully to the words of Demnos and not fall foul of the prickly Federico.

His musings were rudely curtailed as Federico slammed into the room.

'Hieronymous!'

The Count stood in the middle of the room bristling with bad temper.

'You will forgive me for not rising, Count,' replied the soothsayer coolly. He was becoming annoyed by Federico's continual rudeness and bullying manner.

The Count took a pace forward and unsmilingly drew a dagger from his belt.

'Only the dead fail to stand in my presence, Hieronymous. Your lack of courtesy is easily corrected.'

Hieronymous realised he had misread Federico's mood and leapt nimbly to his feet as the dagger moved towards his throat.

'My lord, spare an old servant! It was only through my love for you ... I am numb with fear for your life.'

Federico paused and grinned at the cowering figure of the astrologer.

'But the numbness has passed I see.' He sheathed the dagger and sprawled into a high-backed chair. 'You're a fraud, Hieronymous. A fake. A charlatan. A market-place soothsayer. We both know the truth of it.' He leant forward and poked Hieronymous in the ribs. 'So just remember to keep your humble place, court astrologer. That way you may also keep your head.'

Hieronymous bowed and pulled his beard slyly. 'But I bring you warning, my lord.'

'Go on.'

'There are intrigues brewing. Plots are being prepared. You are in great danger.'

Federico snorted. 'The only plots, astrologer, are mine. And they are going well.'

But Hieronymous continued. 'It is written that a blow will be struck against you—here in this palace. You must bring all your guards here to defend your noble person.'

Federico rose from the chair and thrust the fortune-teller away from him. 'Hieronymous, you try my patience. You can no more read the stars than read my chamber-pot. Go! Get out of my sight!'

Hieronymous's wrinkled face suffused with blood and he swallowed hard in order to control his anger. That this oaf, this ruffian, this mindless brute, regal though he might be, should continually dismiss his predictions as frivolous nonsense was becoming too difficult to stomach.

'Very well, sire,' he replied coldly. 'But before Mars sinks to rest the blow will fall and your life will be forfeit. So it is written.' He delivered the warning with chilling conviction and stalked out of the room leaving Federico puzzled and slightly shaken.

'I'd say you've had visitors,' announced the Doctor as he led the way into Giuliano's room. The staircase had brought them out into the palace kitchens and from there they had been able to reach the sanctuary of the Prince's room unobserved by way of the servants' corridors. The chamber betrayed signs of a fierce struggle. The Prince's telescope had been hurled to the floor but was luckily undamaged.

Giuliano took in the scene, white-faced.

'Marco,' he whispered. 'My uncle's men must have taken him!'

He turned impulsively to the door, ready to set off in search of his companion.

The Doctor restrained him.

'There's nothing you can do on your own Giuliano.' He shut the door gently and led the young Prince to a chair.

'He's my friend, my dear and loyal companion ...'

'Giuliano,' interrupted the Doctor firmly, 'there

are other considerations besides your uncle and his petty ambitions.'

'Petty? But they're far from petty.' Realisation dawned on his face. 'I've called a gathering of scholars to celebrate my accession to the Dukedom. My uncle will do everything he can to stop our meeting.'

This news caused the Doctor to frown. He unhitched his sword and laid it thoughtfully on the table.

'Who's coming to this gathering, Giuliano?'

'The most learned men in all Italy. Scholars, artists, men of the new sciences.'

'Leonardo da Vinci?'

Giuliano nodded. 'And his patron the Duke of Milan.' The Doctor shot a glance at Sarah. She did not seem particularly interested or impressed. Not like her usual curious self. He turned to Giuliano.

'Of course, I see it now. If anything should happen to those men the world would be back in a new dark age!' He crossed to the door. 'You two stay here.'

'Where are you going?' enquired Sarah as if she had suddenly woken up and only heard the last part of their conversation.

'I have an idea who the leader of the brethren is,' replied the Doctor.

'Be careful,' warned Giuliano. 'The soldiers will be everywhere.'

The Doctor beamed a toothy smile. 'Don't worry. Besides I'm not going to pass up the opportunity of meeting Leonardo!' He opened the door and slipped out stealthily into the corridor.

A great bubbling howl of pain echoed through the dungeons of the palace then died away into fitful gasps. The noise came from behind a heavy metal door which gleamed with a dull sheen in the burning torchlight. The sounds stopped, the cell-door opened and the scar-faced captain stepped out. As he turned to close the door Federico slid into view and approached him.

He spoke in a low voice. 'Scarlatti is enjoying his work.'

The captain smiled faintly. 'He is a craftsman.'

'Nonetheless these cries,' the Count gestured towards the cell door, 'I would prefer not to rouse the entire palace.' He pushed his face close to Rossini, his eyes glinting evilly in the dancing shadows. 'Has he weakened yet?'

The captain shook his head, 'He's a stubborn ape, sire.'

Federico thought for a moment. 'I will have a word with him. Sometimes the voice of reason is more effective than a burning iron.' He took Rossini by the shoulder. 'I have another task for you.'

'My lord.'

Federico dropped his voice to a whisper. 'The astrologer, Hieronymous, may be moving against me.' He cast a look up and down the passageway then leant close to Rossini's ear. 'He has prophesied my death.'

'My lord!' Consternation filled the captain's face.

'Don't be alarmed.' Federico waved a hand airily. 'He plucks these lies from the air.' His tone grew stern. 'But I want the old spider out of the city tonight.'

'Banished, sire?'

Federico nodded vigorously. 'Throw him out, and all his rubbish with him.'

The Doctor hurried stealthily through the palace corridors, his feet echoing softly on the marbled floors. It was Sarah who had given him the final clue. She was obviously not herself, under some kind of influence, too subtle to attract Giuliano's attention but sufficient to alert the Doctor. There was only one man capable of practising such tricks, the court astrologer, Hieronymous. The Doctor had had his suspicions for some time but Sarah's disappearance in the catacombs was the convincing link. Hieronymous had to be the leader of the brethren—and in league with the forces of Mandragora. Stop Hieronymous and there was a chance of stopping the invasion of Earth which the Doctor felt sure was imminent. A subtle and insidious invasion, employing the conditioned brethren to dominate and enslave the rest of San Martino, Italy and ultimately the world. Henceforth, mankind would evolve, oblivious to the fact that every act, every word, every thought, emanated from the distant Helix: man's apparent freedom would have turned into a tyranny of the worst kind, the very soul of his existence controlled by another, alien life-form.

The Doctor redoubled his pace, intent on finding Hieronymous's lair. He turned a corner and found himself in a long colonnade. One side bordered a small statue-filled patio, open to the air. As he flitted cautiously from arch to arch he heard a sound as if someone was following him. He dodged into an alcove and waited. He allowed a few moments to pass but there was no further noise. He continued on his way, his ears even more keenly attuned to danger.

Twenty paces behind the Doctor and unknown to him, a pale phantom-like figure tip-toed in his wake. It was Sarah Jane, her eyes peculiarly dilated staring straight ahead, her right hand clenched tightly round the long, pointed bodkin.

'A simple confession, my young friend.' Federico stood

smiling a few feet from Marco, his crooked teeth glinting in the flickering red light. There was a brazier at the far end of the cell into which Scarlatti, the torturer, had thrust two irons. Already they were growing red hot, fit to make a man's flesh sizzle. Marco, his blond hair matted with sweat, hung by his arms from an upright wooden-rack. He turned to face Federico and summoning all his strength gasped a reply.

'Never.'

Federico leant into his ear and whispered silkily. 'You are of noble birth, Marco, a man of intelligence. Use it and save yourself pain.'

'I shall not lie against the Duke.' Marco heaved to gain his breath between each word. 'You may kill me first.'

'No, but we may kill you afterwards. Scarlatti's enthusiasm is such that not all survive his attentions.'

Federico nodded towards the corner. Scarlatti, his shaven head and ox-like arms gleaming with sweat from the heat of the brazier, turned and grinned.

Marco winced. 'You devils . . .'

'One last chance, Marco. Confess that Giuliano is a follower of Demnos. I will reward you well.'

There was no reply. Only numb silence.

'Come, man! What is your answer?' Federico bawled the words out.

Slowly Marco raised his head and deliberately spat into the Count's face.

Federico drew back incensed.

'Insolent fool! Now you will truly learn what suffering is.' He motioned angrily to Scarlatti and stormed out of the cell.

Vexed and embittered from his audience with the Count, Hieronymous had returned to his room and thrown himself into concocting one of his arcane and foul-smelling potions. The noxious fumes rose billowing from the cauldron causing even Hieronymous to cough and splutter and he was forced to open first the window, then the door in order to allow the gases to escape.

In a short while he felt certain the Powers of Mandragora would summon him to embark on the next phase of their mission. Then, Federico would be forced to take heed and eat his rancorous words. Hieronymous stirred the cauldron and threw in a pinch of ground crystals. There was a loud bang and great clouds of steam filled the room. As the air cleared Hieronymous gave a sudden start. Standing before him like a magic apparition was the Doctor.

'Good evening,' he smiled.

Hieronymous gasped. 'You?' His eyes widened in wonder and disbelief. 'What are you?'

'It's time you and I had a serious talk. Hieronymous,' said the Doctor moving round the cauldron.

'Keep back! Keep away from me!'

The Doctor chuckled. 'Not sure of yourself yet. I see—the influence comes and goes, I suppose. That must be very worrying for you.'

The astrologer backed towards the window his arms held in front of his face.

'Were you sent from the stars?'

'You could say that.'

Hieronymous nodded. 'They told me ... the voices ... that I would be joined by another. Give me a proof you are the one.'

The Doctor reached across to the desk and lifted up the carved mask of gold.

'Ingenious. Pre-diluvian sandstone with a complex circuit of base metal fused into it.' He looked up at Hieronymous and grinned. The astrologer was taking no notice and the Doctor realised someone else had entered the room. He dropped the mask and swung round. Less than two paces away Sarah stood poised to plunge a lethal steel needle into the back of his neck.

'You defile the sacred image of Demnos,' screamed Hieronymous. 'Destroy him! Destroy him now!'

9

The Invasion Begins

'Hello, Sarah,' said the Doctor quietly. His eyes took in the bodkin. 'A poisoned needle?'

Sarah hesitated, her arm still raised ready to strike. Her face was like a crazed mask. The Doctor fixed her with a hypnotic stare, his clear blue eyes drilled into hers like a laser beam. 'Drop it, Sarah.'

Hieronymous moved behind him. 'Strike him down!'

Sarah jumped at the Doctor but as the needle flashed towards him he side-stepped and caught hold of her wrist, deflecting the blow.

'You don't want to harm me, Sarah,' he ordered firmly, 'I am your friend. Drop it.'

Sarah struggled for a few seconds, blinked and her face resumed its normal expression. Her gaze fell from the Doctor's eyes to her hand, her fingers opened slowly, and the needle dropped to the ground.

The Doctor smiled gently and released her. As he did so Hieronymous lunged across the room, a dagger in his hand.

'The curse of Demnos on you, forever!'

The Doctor dodged to one side. Hieronymous lunged again. This time the Doctor leant back and neatly kicked the knife out of the astrologer's hand.

'You're really too old for this sort of thing, Hieronymous.'

As the knife went spinning across the floor there was a commotion in the corridor outside and soldiers poured into the room headed by Rossini.

'Take them!'

Three of the guards leapt upon the Doctor who was near the door. He went down struggling.

'Doctor!' yelled Sarah and started clawing at one of the guards.

Hieronymous snatched up the mask. As the soldiers advanced on him he threw a ladle of hot liquid from the cauldron into their faces and dashed behind the curtain at the rear of the chamber. The soldiers fell back screaming and choking.

'Fools! Stop him!' yelled Rossini. 'Don't let him get away.'

But Hieronymous had gained sufficient time to elude them in the darkness of the secret passage and after a brief search the captain had to content himself with his capture of the Doctor and Sarah.

In his private chamber Giuliano was in a flurry of indecision. Sarah had inexplicably slipped out while his back was turned and he had been searching for fresh dressing for his wound.

In addition, there was no word from the Doctor and several hours had passed. He dared not go in search of them for fear of meeting up with Federico's men who were bound to be patrolling the palace. It was pure good fortune they had not returned to search his chambers again and no doubt before the morning they would think of this.

The Prince paced the room for several minutes. Finally he reached a decision. He strapped on his sword belt, crossed to the door and slipped cautiously out into the corridor.

It was still nightfall and the palace lay strangely quiet. Most of the torches had been doused but through the open colonnade a strong moonlight cast a pale ethereal glow onto the marbled floor. For some reason the quiet cool atmosphere made him think back to his childhood, how as a little boy he had often played alone in these same corridors dreaming of the day he would be crowned Duke and ruler of San Martino. And now that day had come here he was, a fugitive in his own house, fearing for his life, with only the strange and resourceful Doctor as his ally.

He padded stealthily down the corridors heading for Hieronymous's chamber. He felt sure that was where the Doctor had meant to visit.

Suddenly there was a blur of movement behind a column to his right and two shadowy figures hurled themselves upon him. A knee dug him savagely in the back and before he could draw his sword a sharp blade was pressed to his throat. Then swiftly his assailants dragged him out of the corridor and down a flight of stone steps.

'Giuliano?'

Federico's ugly face lit up and he rose eagerly from his couch to greet Rossini.

'Is he dead?'

'No, sire. He's been taken to the dungeon with the other prisoners.'

'Then it is finished, Rossini!' The Count rubbed his hands and began prowling his chamber in a fit of excitement. 'The Duke and his troublemakers will be dead and buried by cockcrow.' Rossini bowed obediently. 'There is only Hieronymous. But he will not evade capture for long.'

Federico nodded fervently, 'There is nothing now that will stop me. Nothing!' He turned to Rossini, his face ablaze with triumph.

In the dungeons the Doctor and Sarah hung side by side on vertical wooden racks, their wrists manacled to the frame above their heads. They had been placed in Marco's cell and the heat of the brazier caused the sweat to pour off them, adding to their discomfort. Opposite them Marco hung limp and motionless, his blond hair matted, his face streaked with tears and dirt. Only a faint panting from time to time told them he was still alive.

Sarah turned her head with difficulty and whispered faintly to the Doctor.

'I'm trying to remember what happened to me but I can't. There's nothing at all.'

'Drug-induced hypnosis,' replied the Doctor, easing himself free from the wooden slats which seemed to be eating through his shoulder-blades. 'Hieronymous is a resourceful old sly-boots.'

Sarah looked sad and puzzled.

'But I tried to kill you?'

'You only did what you were ordered to do—and what I expected,' said the Doctor without reproach.

'But how did you know I'd been drugged?'

'Well I've taken you to some strange places and you've never stopped to wonder why you spoke the local language. It's a Timelord gift that I let you share.

87

But tonight you asked how you could understand Italian.'

'Did I?'

'Yes. And that told me your mind had been taken over by another influence.'

Sarah was about to question the Doctor further when the bolt was drawn back with a clank, and Giuliano was led in between two soldiers. He gasped at the sight of the Doctor and Sarah.

'See to Marco,' urged the Doctor.

Giuliano darted to his companion's side and cupped his head in his hands.

'Marco? What have they done to you?'

Marco's eyelids flickered momentarily and his lips trembled. 'They made me ... speak against you.' His chin fell heavily to his chest with the effort. Pity and anger mingled on Giuliano's face as he stared upon his boyhood companion.

'What have they forced you to say?' he whispered.

'That you, dear nephew,' answered a gloating voice from behind, 'and this dog of a sorcerer are in league to revive the blasphemous cult of Demnos.'

Giuliano swung round on his heels to encounter the towering figure of his uncle, arms folded and legs astride, leering devilishly at him from the doorway.

'You stinking butcher!'

Giuliano sprang at Federico's throat but the two soldiers wrenched him away and held him tight. The Count chuckled and, removing his gauntlet, struck his nephew playfully across the cheek.

Behind him Rossini entered hastily.

'My lord.'

'What is it?'

The captain was pale and breathless. 'All over the city ... they're coming out of every street ...'

'What are you gabbling about?'

'The brethren,' gasped Rossini. 'They're moving towards the temple!'

Through the empty streets hordes of sinister wraith-like figures glided over the cobblestones like a surging tide. Rossini, who had witnessed the spectacle from the upper window in the palace, ten minutes earlier, had never seen such a sight. No one, not even Federico had realised the brethren numbered so many.

At the southern end of the city files of black hooded figures merged into one large column and surged across the Slopes of Sorrow towards the ruined temple.

Inside the sacrificial chamber, Hieronymous, cloaked in purple and wearing the golden mask, stood at the foot of the altar as the brethren arrived and took up their positions. By his side stood the High Priest, adorned for the first time in a tall silver mask fashioned like a gargoyle.

Once the brethren were fully assembled a low chanting commenced, which gradually rose in volume as they began processing around the central altar. After a few moments Hieronymous climbed onto the top step of the altar, and kneeling down, kissed the base of the stone. Then raising his arms exultantly he called out in an unknown tongue.

Immediately, a strange shimmering effect appeared on the walls of the cavern and the sound of creaking, grinding stone-work echoed above the heads of the brethren. Slowly and majestically the outline of their former temple materialised around them. When the shape was complete and the noise had ceased Hieronymous rose to his feet and made another gesture, bringing his arms down to his sides in a wide circling motion.

As he did so a brilliant shaft of light bathed him and the altar in a curious ethereal glow. The centre of the column of light was an intense iridescent white, impossible to look upon directly, fading towards the outer edges into a vivid spectrum of colours, orange, green, vermilion, and peacock-blue.

The chanting from the brethren ceased and Hieronymous cried in a loud voice.

'Great God Demnos, we are ready to receive you into ourselves. If we are worthy of your almighty presence, show yourself.'

For a few moments nothing happened, then a mighty lightning flash like a shooting star sped down the beam of light and struck the altar where Hieronymous was standing!

Instantly he turned into a vivid ball of colour as the charge travelled straight through him, from head to foot. Miraculously, he remained alive and intact. As if obeying some unheard command he spread his gloved hands over the altar, about a foot above the surface. Immediately a force of energy leapt from the stone to his hands and his fingers crackled with blue light. He beckoned to the High Priest who approached from the other side of the altar and raised his hands. Hieronymous took hold of them in his and a bolt of energy passed through into the High Priest. He jerked convulsively as if a powerful electric current had entered his body. Hieronymous released his grip and the High Priest stepped back to his position.

The process had begun. The first recipients of Mandragora's awesome power had relinquished their human selves.

If Rossini's news was true then there was even less time than the Doctor had first thought. It was imperative to convince Federico of the imminent danger. But the cunning tyrant was determined to enjoy his moment of glory.

'I've waited a long time, sorcerer, for this moment. Nothing is going to stop me now from becoming Duke.'

The Doctor retorted angrily. 'Count Federico, I'm not interested in your political ambitions. Your enemies are not here in this dungeon, they're in the temple. It's not Giuliano you have to fear but Hieronymous.'

Federico snorted. 'Hieronymous? That old fake?'

'That old fake, Count, is the leader of the brethren.'

'What?' Federico's cheeks drained of what little colour they had and he stared uncomprehendingly at Rossini.

'And he's possessed of some extraordinary power,' continued the Doctor smoothly, 'Helix Energy. It's a power that could destroy everything. I've warned you before.'

'It's a trick, sire.'

Federico looked from the captain to the Doctor, in two minds.

'How do I know sorcerer, that you are telling the truth?'

'You don't. But if you don't stop Hieronymous, now, I promise you there'll be no Dukedom for you or anyone else to rule over after tonight.'

The Count looked visibly shaken. He hesitated a moment then said, 'I'll see for myself. And you'll come with me.' He prodded the Doctor in the ribs. 'Unchain him.'

'Don't trust him, my lord,' remonstrated the captain.

Federico sneered.

'I don't have to trust him. Keep these three as hostages.' He indicated Giuliano, Sarah and the still half-conscious Marco. 'If I don't return within the hour you know what to do.'

Rossini clicked his heels and nodded and the guards began unchaining the Doctor. Sarah looked anxiously at Giuliano. There was nothing they could do. The Doctor was taking the only course open to him. Their lives once more lay in his hands—and Federico's.

In the temple the brethren were still filing slowly up to the altar one by one and receiving the 'energy charge' from Hieronymous. Those who had already undergone the ordeal stood silently in the centre of the chamber, their masked faces trained obediently on their leader. They seemed no longer human, too stiff, too still, like row upon row of carved dummies.

As the altar queue gradually dwindled a handful of latecomers appeared and tagged on the end. Their hoods were pulled far forward concealing their faces and they quickly mingled in with the other brethren as if not wanting to attract attention. They were a good fifty feet away from the altar when Hieronymous suddenly looked up from his administrations and stared in their direction. The tallest of the latecomers whispered in his neighbour's ear.

'Don't go near him.'

'Do I need your advice?' snarled Federico and motioned his guards to keep a firm grip on the Doctor's arms. Then, suddenly throwing back his hood he ran towards the altar and pointed an accusing finger.

'Hieronymous! You traitor!'

The masked figure whirled round. Federico signalled to his men to seize the astrologer. The guards started to obey then stopped in their tracks. They seemed frozen with fear, transfixed by the devilish staring mask.

'Hieronymous!'

Federico rushed forward, screaming with fury. An inner demon drove him on to seek vengeance on his old astrologer. He leapt up the altar steps and tore the golden mask from Hieronymous's face. Instantly he fell back in horror. There was no face behind the mask! No flesh, no bone, nothing. Nothing but a blinding searing light framed by the edges of the black hood. It was clear there was nothing beneath the cloak, no person at all, just a power source in the shape of a man.

The 'Shape' raised its arm and pointed a gloved finger at Federico. The Count cringed in terror. The Doctor looked on in horrified fascination, unable to intervene. The gloved finger levelled at Federico's heart and daggers of blue light spurted from the tip striking him instantly. Federico gave a hideous shriek and exploded into a mass of flames. His guards ran to his aid but they too were instantly devoured by a burst from Hieronymous's outstretched arm.

The Doctor turned pale as he gazed at the charred and smoking pile which an instant before had been Count Federico. The effects of Mandragora Energy were more lethal than a laser beam, more powerful than nuclear fission. And in this temple a multitude were already armed with the same weapon. Unless he could escape, Earth was doomed. Had his alien presence yet been detected by the intelligences of Mandragora? As if in reply the gloved finger of Hieronymous swung sharply round and pointed ominously in the Doctor's direction.

10

Siege

For a moment the Doctor felt his heart stop beating. Time stood still and it seemed to him as if the sum total of his existence lay naked and defenceless before that threatening accusing finger. He closed his eyes and waited.

'So shall perish all our earthly enemies.'

The voice of Hieronymous echoed exultantly round the cavernous chamber. The Doctor opened one eye. The masked figure had lowered its arm and now addressed the enraptured brethren.

'Surround me with the Helix of power, brothers, and none can overcome us.' Hieronymous lowered his head reverentially and sank into a kneeling position. The Doctor stood in a daze of relief as the brothers nearest to him jostled and pressed their way towards the base of the altar.

There they formed a circle and began a low chant while Hieronymous continued to address them with messianic fervour.

'All has happened as was foretold down the centuries. The waiting, the prayers, the sacrifices. Now, at last, the Empire of Mandragora will encompass the Earth. For Demnos is only the servant of Mandragora and Mandragora is the mighty master of all things.'

The Doctor looked cautiously about him. Everyone seemed preoccupied, So, bowing his head and mumbling furtively he took his chance and backed away towards the nearest exit. Luckily it was the one through which Federico's men had gained admittance. He knew he could remember the way out.

'Let the power flood into you, brothers. Tonight we shall witness the last prophesy.'

The Doctor reached the shadows. Hieronymous raised his voice. 'As it is written, Mandragora shall swallow the moon. Then shall we strike!'

The masked figure leapt to his feet and made a sweeping gesture with his fist.

The Doctor raised an eyebrow, interested. Battle plans? Of a sort, yes, but puzzling. Now was not the time to work them out.

Swiftly and stealthily he left the sacrificial chamber and retraced his steps towards the palace.

In the dungeons Sarah, Giuliano and Marco hung manacled to their racks just as Federico had ordered. Marco had now regained consciousness but was still in a bad way. Rossini stood staring at him without sympathy flanked by four armed guards. From time to time he prodded the red-hot irons in the brazier, more out of idle curiosity than from any desire to use them. Even so it was enough to alarm Sarah who was not accustomed to hanging around in medieval torture chambers.

The Doctor had been gone over an hour when a fifth guard appeared in the doorway and bowed at Rossini. The scar-faced captain nodded and turned to his captives.

'It is time. Count Federico ordered that these traitors be executed at the end of an hour.'

'Only if he didn't return,' protested Sarah.

'Neither he nor the sorcerer nor any of their party have returned from the temple,' replied the captain flatly.

'You mean it's an hour already? Doesn't time fly when you're having fun.'

Rossini motioned to his guards. 'Take them down.'

The guard nearest Giuliano began to undo his manacles.

'Stay, fellow,' commanded the Prince. 'Rossini, you call us traitors, but lay a hand on your Prince and you will be the traitor.'

The guard hesitated, uncertain what to do.

'I follow the Count.' replied Rossini gruffly.

'You follow a tyrant and a murderer!' gasped Marco from his pallet. 'It is Giuliano to whom you owe allegiance.'

'Enough!' cried Rossini. 'Take them down! The execution block grows dry.'

The guards bowed and hurriedly released the prisoners from their wooden racks.

'Infamous filth!' groaned Marco as he staggered to keep upright. 'Call yourselves soldiers!'

His hands freed, Giuliano stood proud and erect facing his captors. 'Are we to die without even a priest?'

'Or a hearty breakfast?' chipped in Sarah.

'No priest available,' said a voice from the door. 'Will a brother do?'

They all spun round to see the Doctor framed in the doorway beaming, the brother's cowl pushed back from his face.

Rossini was the first to recover. 'What have you done to the Count, sorcerer?' he snarled.

'Federico is dead.'

Giuliano turned pale. 'Dead? My uncle is dead?'

The Doctor nodded. 'In the temple ruins.'

'How did he die?'

'Let's just say Hieronymous gave him a blank look.'

Rossini began to tremble and the weal-mark on his cheek grew purple. He pointed to the Doctor angrily. 'Seize him!'

But the soldiers hung back, stunned by the news of Federico's death.

'Seize him!'

The guards still did not move.

'Rossini, you don't have any authority now,' said the Doctor. 'There's your lawful ruler.' He turned to Giuliano.

Giuliano addressed the bewildered soldiers. 'You men. Are you with your Prince?'

There was a moment's pause then all five soldiers uncovered their heads and knelt before the Prince. Rossini, left standing, lowered his eyes then followed suit.

'Take him to the block!'

'No, Marco,' replied the Prince restraining his companion. He nodded to the soldiers. 'Take him away. I'll decide his fate later.'

The newly-converted guards rose and, taking hold of Rossini, marched him out of the cell.

Marco sprang to the Prince's side and clasped him about the neck. 'Giuliano, the evil is ended! At last you can rule without fear.'

'Wrong, Marco,' interrupted the Doctor. 'The evil is only just beginning. Hieronymous and the brethren still remain.'

'Then destroy them, my lord,' urged Marco. 'You must take command!'

Giuliano paused, taking stock. 'Is that what you think, Doctor?'

'You are the Prince! The soldiers will rally to you. Lead them to this temple, win your inheritance, sire.'

The Doctor smiled. 'Marco, Marco.' He took him by the shoulders and led him gently to a bench. Then, turning to Giuliano he said, 'If you go near that temple you go to your death.'

Giuliano looked uncertain. 'Then what do you suggest? What would you have me do?'

The Doctor glanced at the open doorway to make sure no one was listening.

'The brethren are still absorbing power. Get every man you can, soldiers, joiners, stonemasons, and block all entrances to the palace. Turn it into a fortress,' he looked earnestly into the Prince's face. 'Because when the brethren come here, you're going to need one.'

Supporting his companion Giuliano led him out of the cell towards the upper palace.

Sarah turned to the Doctor. 'Are the barricades enough to stop the brethren?' she asked gently.

'Anything to delay them, Sarah. I need time to think. Anyway his power isn't complete yet.' The Doctor unclipped his cloak and threw it aside. 'Come on.' He headed out of the cell.

'What do you mean?' called Sarah as she followed him out of the dungeons and up a stone staircase. The Doctor prised open a thick studded door at the top and poked his head through. He beckoned her on and the two of them stepped gingerly into the moonlit colonnade running alongside the state rooms.

'This way,' whispered the Doctor, and then continued to explain. 'So far the only Helix Energy available in the brethren is what we brought with us.'

'Well that's bad enough,' Sarah frowned. 'You mean there's more to come?' The Doctor nodded. 'Tomorrow night. When Mandragora swallows the moon.'

Sarah stopped, hands on hips. 'Listen, I came here with you remember? You don't have to use that fifteenth-century double talk with me. I speaka da pretty good English.'

'I was just repeating what he said,' replied the Doctor and disappeared smartly behind a stone column. Sarah had to run to catch up. 'Who?'

The Doctor hurried on, checking carefully at each corridor intersection before hopping across.

'Hieronymous. When Mandragora swallows the moon they're going to strike.'

Sarah sighed in frustration.

'But what does it mean?'

The Doctor did not answer. They had come to a halt outside an imposing door with the royal crest of arms carved in wood and gilt above. Sarah recognised it as the entrance to Giuliano's chambers. The Doctor pushed the door open and ventured in. The room was empty. Quickly he moved to the window and began dismantling Giuliano's telescope which still stood at an angle on the table where Marco had left it. He squinted through the eyepiece at Sarah.

'Just about adequate I suppose.' He adjusted the focus. 'Another fifty years and we could have used Galileo's. Come on.' He was at the door and off again before she'd had time to draw breath.

'Where are you going now?' protested Sarah, but he had already gone and she knew she would have to follow to find out. The Doctor in one of his impulsive moods was always the same. She pulled a wry face and set off after him.

Elsewhere in the palace there was great activity. The main gates leading onto the city square had been barricaded and all side entrances to the royal mansion were being sealed off. Giuliano himself was busy commanding the work from the corridor outside the state rooms.

As he ordered a group of stonemasons and carpenters to the west gate Marco ran up. He had changed into fresh clothes, but still looked weakened from his ordeal.

'Sire, it's begun!'

'What?'

'The brethren. They are driving people from the town.'

Giuliano's handsome features darkened at this information. 'Are you sure of this?'

Marco nodded. 'Those who refuse to leave are being destroyed by bolts of fire. They have brought the forces of darkness out of those devilish catacombs.'

The young Prince pushed open the doors leading to the state rooms and led his companion inside. If overheard, the news could spread alarm and panic.

'So we are isolated now,' deliberated Giuliano, 'just the few of us in this palace.'

'Some of them the most precious heads in all Europe, sire.'

Giuliano sank into the high backed throne and Marco read the gravity of the situation in his master's bleak expression.

'Do they know what we face?'

'I think they have some fear that all is not well,' replied Marco. 'Their personal guards stay close. And the King of Naples asked the reason for all the noise. I sent back word that it was a preparation for the masque.'

Giuliano leapt to his feet. 'The masque! I had forgotten the day. Marco, it must be cancelled.'

Marco shook his head. 'Would you explain to your peers that your accession to the throne cannot be celebrated because of a pagan uprising?'

'The masque cannot be held, Marco! It is too dangerous.' The young Prince grew flushed and agitated.

'I have seen our defences, sire,' replied Marco calmly. 'This palace could be held against an army. And the brothers are not an army, they are a fanatical rabble.'

'Who can kill with bolts of fire.'

'Simple trickery. Hieronymous was always a cunning fox. And do not forget, my lord, we have weapons of our own.' Giuliano looked hard into the eyes of his steadfast companion. All the years he had known him he had proved a wise and loyal counsellor. But now they were dealing with powers and events outside their knowledge. He wondered how his father the old duke would have reacted, how would he best have protected his people? And for the first time realised the awesome burden of office that was his inheritance. 'I don't know, Marco,' the young Prince hesitated.

His companion grasped him by the shoulders. 'Giuliano, you are the ruler now. A leader. If you falter at the first challenge, you may lose everything. There are eyes watching. There are those who will go from here saying the Duke of San Martino is weak, ready to be toppled. Better to trust your guards and hold the masque as though all were normal.'

For several moments the young Prince did not respond. Then clasping Marco's arms in his, he smiled. 'You speak sense as always, dear Marco, but all is not normal. You and I both know it. I will seek the Doctor's advice. Where is he?'

'In Hieronymous's room. He has been there since this morning. But what he does there I know not.'

'Astrolabe, Sarah.' The Doctor held out a hand.

'What?'

'The astrolabe,' repeated the Doctor sharply. He was perched on a stool his right eye firmly glued to Giuliano's telescope which pointed skywards out of the window. He waggled his fingers. 'The medieval sextant.'

'Oh.' Sarah scratched her head and selected the most likely contender from the curious instruments which lay scattered about the chamber. 'What exactly are you trying to do, Doctor?'

'I'm trying to get this thing to work. Exactly. Roughly will be no good at all.' He levelled the sextant towards the sun. 'Unfortunately, the alidade is almost a whole degree out.' He adjusted the brass screw on the side of the sextant, took a sighting and began a rapid calculation.

'Compensate for error, then convert to the Copernican system, hundred and twenty degrees, that's eight, and seventeen from sixty ...'

'Forty-three.'

'Forty-three, thank you Sarah, that's ... that's it. I've done it.' He beamed. 'Eight minutes and forty-three seconds after nine o'clock tonight.'

'What?'

'Mandragora swallows the moon. In other words, a lunar eclipse.'

'And that's when the brethren will attack?'

The Doctor nodded. 'I imagine so. More important,' he gestured around the room, 'it's when all this paraphernalia could become man's only science.'

Sarah pulled a face. 'Astrology? You mean when Mars is in the house of the ram and all that nonsense?'

'Nonsense?' retorted the Doctor. 'It's not nonsense.' He wagged a finger at Sarah. 'Remember Hieronymous, what he did to you. The Mandragorans don't conquer in a physical sense. They dominate and control by Helix Energy, astral influence. They take away the one thing worth having.'

'Which is?'

'The essence of life. Purpose. The ability granted to every intelligent species to shape its destiny.' The Doctor stepped down from the window, animated by his concern. 'Once let them gain control and man's ambition will never stretch beyond the next meal. They'll turn you into sheep. Idle, useless, mindless sheep.' He paused, his voice raised and angry at the thought.

Sarah held up her hands. 'All right. I'm convinced.' It was not often the Doctor grew so heated or showed his true feelings. Sarah often wondered why he cared so much for Earth and its people. But she knew it was the principle which counted. It was oppression and tyranny he fought. Whether on a small scale with Federico and San Martino, or Mandragora and Earth, it amounted to the same denial of freedom.

'But what can we do?' she asked finally. There was no reply from the Doctor. He had adopted the familiar lotus position of an Eastern mystic, eyes closed, hands pressed firmly together, and now sat immobile in the middle of the room. Instead there was a tap at the door and Giuliano entered accompanied by a soldier.

'I'd like ...' Giuliano broke off and stared at the Doctor.

'Don't worry,' explained Sarah, 'he's only thinking.'

The Doctor let out a loud snore.

'Thinking?' queried the Prince.

Sarah frowned. 'I think.'

'I came to seek his advice.'

The Doctor suddenly opened his eyes and bounced to his feet. 'All or nothing, Sarah. I'll have to take a gamble.' He started towards the door.

'Doctor,' said Giuliano, intercepting him.

'Hello.' The Doctor flashed a quick smile. 'If it's ionised plasma it's molecular, i.e. there's only a certain amount of it. And by now it must be spread pretty thinly among Hieronymous and the brethren. Exhaust it. That's the answer!' He beamed triumphantly at Giuliano.

'Doctor, I have a question.'

The Doctor tapped the soldier's chainmail jerkin.

'Can you get me one of these? And a good length of wire?'

'Wire?' Giuliano looked bewildered.

'Yes wire! Good heavens, man, it's at least a hundred and fifty years since wire-drawing machines were invented. You must have some about the place.'

The Prince gave a baffled shrug. 'If you would speak to the palace armourer ...'

'Of course, yes! I'll see him right away.' The Doctor strode to the door then turned, remembering something. 'Did you have a question?'

'I wanted to speak to you about tonight's masque— the ball for all our distinguished visitors,' replied Giuliano. 'Everything is arranged, but it could yet be cancelled.'

The Doctor chuckled. 'Oh I see. You're going to have a hop? How splendid!'

'If you don't think it's too dangerous,' ventured Giuliano tentatively.

'Dangerous?' The Doctor shook his head vigorously. 'Duke, you have a lot of guests to entertain. Of course you must hold the masque. Sarah will love it.' He waved an arm and disappeared.

'Oh yes,' said Sarah with heavy sarcasm, 'it'll be just my scene!'

The Doctor popped his head round the door again. 'And save me a costume, Giuliano, I love a good knees up.' Then he was gone.

Sarah was forced to laugh at the young Duke's perplexed expression. She had forgotten how unsettling the Doctor's bouts of enthusiasm could be to anyone who didn't know him.

Hieronymous stood alone on the topmost step of the altar, his golden mask glinting in the flickering torchlight. Behind the eye-slits in the mask, where once the astrologer's own beady eyes looked out, was now a dim pulsating glow. The purple gloves still covered his long, extended fingers.

There was a movement in the shadows and the High Priest, also masked, ascended the altar steps.

Hieronymous inclined his head. 'The hour fast approaches.'

'What is your plan, Great One?'

The High Priest's voice echoed through the sepulchral gloom. No longer human, it sounded hoarse, devoid of emotion, like dry leaves rustling in the wind.

'The plan of Mandragora,' answered Hieronymous. 'I am but the vessel for those who hold dominion over the cosmos.'

'The mighty sky gods? What would they have us do, lord?'

Hieronymous turned to face the High Priest and the eye-slits in his ghoulish mask grew red and fierce.

'This time and place were well chosen. Assembled in the palace are many scholars, men of science and learning, many rulers and nobles. Tonight they are to be destroyed. All of them. In this way shall be established the power and supremacy of those masters we serve.'

The High Priest bowed.

'The Duke has deployed many soldiers. All the entrances to the palace are fortified and heavily guarded, lord.'

Hieronymous dropped his voice to a whisper. 'There is still an entrance they know nothing of. Bring me ten of the brethren. I will take them to the palace.' He leant closer to his acolyte's ear. 'Tonight there is a masque in the Duke's honour. We will provide the entertainers!'

The High Priest bowed low and backed away into the shadows. As he did so a peculiar croaking noise emanated from behind the grinning mask of Hieronymous, like a hideous inhuman cackle.

11

Duel to the Death

In Giuliano's room the Doctor was endeavouring to get into the chainmail jerkin. He tugged and heaved at the weighty garment, struggling to fasten it round his bulky frame. The jerkin was the largest the palace possessed but still it was a tight fit. At last he managed it with the help of the palace armourer and a good deal of ill-tempered muttering.

'Now the coat. I don't want it to show.'

The armourer helped the Doctor into his velvet frock-coat shaking his head in bewilderment at this eccentric and unorthodox procedure.

At this moment Sarah entered the room her arms laden with a number of fancy dress costumes.

'How do I look?' enquired the Doctor anxiously.

Sarah walked up to him and prodded his stomach. 'Are you putting on weight?' The Doctor looked hurt. 'And what's that in aid of?' She yanked the metal jerkin.

'A little plan.' The Doctor turned to the armourer. 'Leave the wire.'

The armourer bowed, placed a long coil of metal wire on the sword-chest and then left.

Sarah held out the costumes. 'Giuliano sent you these to choose from.'

The Doctor selected a baggy russet-coloured garment with a large lion's head. 'This is rather dignified, don't you think?' The Doctor donned the lion's head and let out a roar.

'I think it's ridiculous to be talking about fancy dress—I mean if we're in such desperate danger.'

The Doctor pawed the air with his hands, threw back his lion's mane and roared again.

'Oh stop it!' cried Sarah, genuinely upset.

'Remember the French before Agincourt?' The lion's head waggled stupidly.

Sarah turned away. There were times when the Doctor's behaviour infuriated her. 'One thing I've noticed about you,' she said bitterly, 'the worse the situation the worse your jokes get.'

The Doctor stopped his fooling abruptly and removed the costume head.

'I'll settle for the lion, all right?' he said quickly.

Sarah eyed him seriously. 'Things are bad, aren't they?'

'Yes.' The Doctor picked up the wire.

'Very bad?'

The Doctor nodded. 'Desperately bad. We can only do our best—and hope.' His blue eyes met Sarah's and for once they lacked their natural warmth and sparkle. In that moment Sarah knew they were up against something far more powerful and frightening than even she had dared imagine.

The Doctor took her hand. 'Coming?'

She smiled weakly and followed him out.

In the state rooms and adjoining ante-chambers the guests were already trickling in prior to the masque commencing. The musicians were tuning up in the balcony and kitchen boys scurried hither and thither with last minute additions to the huge banqueting table which ran along one side of the ballroom.

The Doctor and Sarah arrived in one of the anterooms with Marco. The Doctor clutched the lion's head. On a bench beneath a window were seated three bizarre figures in fancy dress, a goat's head in white alabaster with snarling nostrils and fiercesome horns, an oxen with gaping jaws, and an ogling clown with bloated cheeks and stringy hair falling around its shoulders. The Doctor drew Marco's attention to the monstrous trio.

'Is Leonardo da Vinci among that lot?'

Marco smiled. 'Those are the entertainers.'

The Doctor shook his head, disappointed. 'I don't think I'm ever going to see Leonardo, Sarah.' He addressed Marco again.

'Have the dungeon entrance opened.'

'I'll see to it at once, Doctor.' Marco sped away.

The Doctor turned to Sarah. 'I want you to stay here and keep an eye on this lot.'

'What for?' protested Sarah.

'A Time Lord has to do what a Time Lord has to do.' He lifted the coil of wire. 'Besides, you're not equipped.'

They had reached the colonnade which led down to the dungeons.

'Doctor, you said it was dangerous.'

'Did I? Oh, yes.'

'Well is it dangerous?'

'Only if I've guessed wrong.'

Sarah caught hold of the Doctor's arm and forced him to a halt. 'I wish you'd stop giving me flip answers!'

'All right.' The Doctor turned and faced her. 'Cosmic rays—negatively charged high-energy particles—follow magnetic lines of force. So, if I've guessed right about the nature of Helix Energy, I should be able to drain it off.'

Sarah nodded. 'And if you're wrong?'

The Doctor smiled expansively. 'When have I ever been wrong about anything?' He gave her a sly wink and disappeared down the corridor.

Sarah stared after his retreating figure and bit her lip. 'Lots of times,' she said to herself quietly and there was a look of sadness in her eyes.

In the temple ruins a figure slid into the Sacrificial Chamber and approached the purple form of Hieronymous standing sentinel-like beside the altar.

'The masque has begun,' reported the High Priest urgently. 'Shall I order our brothers into position?'

'Yes. Kill all who try to escape.'

'The others are inside?'

'Concealed from prying eyes. They await only my signal.'

The High Priest bowed. 'Glory to Demnos.'

'And to Mandragora.'

The High Priest bowed once more and glided away into the shadows. Hieronymous watched him disappear, then strutted majestically down from the altar and vanished through a hidden exit.

A few moments later a grinning lion's head peered round a broken column, and the Doctor stepped out. He glanced quickly round the cavernous chamber to make sure he was alone. Then, laying aside the lion's head, he unwound the coil of wire and began scrabbling about in the dirt at the base of the altar.

In the palace the state rooms were now full of guests as the masque began. The visiting dignitaries were easy to pick out in their sumptuous costumes, each with a clutch of courtiers swaggering and prancing around them in exaggerated fashion. Every guest wore a mask or disguise of some kind and there was much chaffing and banter as young gallants tried to guess the identity of their pretty partners.

After one or two lively opening dances the musicians delivered a roll on the drums and through the large double doors tottered a motley clad jester on tall wooden stilts. There were 'oohs' and 'ahs' of delight as he wobbled about the floor, towering over the frightened lady courtiers. Then with a shout he leapt from the stilts and somersaulted up onto a trestled table. Plucking three lighted torches from the wall, he began to juggle with them high in the air.

Giuliano looked on from a raised dais at the far end of the room, a faint smile on his lips. He was doing his best to be outwardly calm and courteous to his visitors, but his thoughts were on the hidden danger that lay outside. As he nodded politely to the Duke and Duchess of Milan he caught sight of Marco anxiously pushing towards him through the crowd.

'Sire!'

'What is it?'

'I have heard a report from the guards. The brethren ...'

Giuliano hushed his companion and drew him to one side. 'What of them?'

'They are all round the outside of the palace. It is as though they are waiting for something.'

Giuliano looked puzzled. 'What could it be—a signal?'

Marco shrugged. 'Perhaps. They are just standing silently in the shadows.'

The Prince broke off to applaud the juggler. 'Is Hieronymous with them?'

'He has not been seen, my lord.'

'I don't like the smell of it, Marco.' Giuliano gestured towards the floor. 'Even our guests sense that something is wrong. See how quiet they are.'

Marco followed his gaze and it was true. Small knots of guests, close advisers of visiting Heads of State, were muttering quietly to one another and casting anxious looks about the room.

Marco grasped the young Duke's arm encouragingly. 'Giuliano, take heart. Our walls are thick and solid and the guards well-trained—a match for any in the land. At least we have your uncle to thank for that.'

'You think we have nothing to fear?'

'I think by dawn Hieronymous will have realised his mistake. He and his followers will leave San Martino to search for easier pickings elsewhere.'

'I hope you are right,' replied Giuliano but he seemed unconvinced.

There was a cry of amazement from the guests clustered about the juggler as he reached the finale of his act, thrusting a blazing torch into his mouth without apparent harm. Giuliano rose to his feet and led the applause. Marco followed suit and the two of them descended from the dais onto the dance floor.

'Sire, if needs be,' continued Marco, 'we can hold out here for a month. And long before that the armies of neighbouring states would come to our help.'

Giuliano acknowledged his friend's counsel then smiled and bowed to a pretty young lady who approached. She wore a beautiful satin gown of exquisite pearl grey and a filigree silver mask covered her eyes. Giuliano was especially taken with the delicate nape of her neck, her lustrous hair, and found himself strongly attracted to this mysterious stranger.

'Have you seen the Doctor?' she asked, and Giuliano realised with a shock it was the Doctor's companion, Sarah.

'No,' he answered endeavouring to regain his composure.

Sarah seemed oblivious to the effect she had caused. 'He should be here by now,' she said impatiently. 'It must be nearly nine.'

'It was eight of the evening when I toured the guards,' answered Marco.

'This waiting, not knowing what's happening, is worse than being with him.' Sarah scoured the dancing throng but the Doctor was nowhere to be seen. As she stood on the edge of the dancers a Florentine gallant stepped forward and made a low bow before her.

'Who, me?' responded Sarah, looking round to see if she was mistaken. The gallant bowed again, even lower this time. Sarah shrugged and took his hand. As the young gallant minced off with his prize Sarah threw Giuliano a desperate look. The handsome young Duke raised an eyebrow and smiled.

As Sarah whirled elegantly about the dance floor she caught sight of the hideous features of the entertainers standing motionless in the corners of the room, the goat, the oxen, and the clown, and for some reason the sight of them sent an icy chill down her spine.

The Doctor was crouched low by a corner of the altar finishing off his work. He had run the wire right round the base of the altar, in contact with it, to form a circuit. From this he had led off a number of 'spokes' to the area immediately surrounding the altar and camouflaged the whole skein of wires with earth and stones. The remaining wire he attached to the chain jerkin beneath his coat, leaving the other end free to trail on the ground. Then, satisfied, he leant casually against the altar and dusted his hands.

He had his back to the hidden exit. Instinct told him that Hieronymous would return, before the final assault, to gain inspiration and strength of purpose from the sacred stone. And in that short time the Doctor knew he had to make his move, draw Hieronymous and the Helix Energy into a deadly and decisive confrontation, or else all was lost.

Sure enough, after a few minutes, he heard the sound of someone picking their way through the ruins towards him. The muscles in the Doctor's face tensed but he kept his relaxed posture.

'You profane the sacred stone.'

The voice was deathly, menacing, war-like.

The Doctor turned casually. 'Hello there! Had a hard day in the catacombs?'

'You profane the sacred stone!'

'Come now! You know who I am.' The Doctor spread his arms in a friendly gesture. 'You can drop all that bosh about stones and profanity. Just be your natural horrid self.'

Hieronymous halted about twelve feet away. The eye-slits of his mask seemed ablaze in the dark shadows of the cavern. 'Why have you come here, Time Lord?'

'Well I had no choice, you see,' replied the Doctor, deliberately fudging the issue.

'Had it not been you, there would have been other travellers drawn into the Mandragora Helix. Earth had to be possessed.' The purple gloved hands reached out in a clenching, grasping motion. 'Unchecked, man's curiosity might lead him away from this planet until, ultimately, even the galaxy itself may not contain him! We of Mandragora will not permit a rival power within our dominion!'

'Pity,' said the Doctor, 'because I can't allow you to interfere with Earth's progress.'

'You arrogant dolt!' Hieronymous advanced threateningly. 'How dare you oppose the might of Mandragora!'

'I'm afraid it's part of a Time Lord's job to insist on justice for all species.'

'Then you will be swept aside like the dirt that you are.'

'Really?' The Doctor backed away carefully down the altar steps. He knew that any second now Hieronymous could point his finger and the lethal bolts would be unleashed, and he wanted to be in the correct position.

Suddenly, Hieronymous rushed towards him, the horrible, contorted visage illuminated by the red-hot energy force within.

'Die, Doctor!' he screamed and, raising his right arm, fired a bolt of Helix Energy straight at the Doctor.

There was a bright flash and the Doctor felt a massive jolt in his chest like a powerful electric shock. He staggered backwards but managed to regain his balance.

'Time Lords don't die so easily,' he gasped through gritted teeth.

Hieronymous moved in closer for the kill.

'We shall crush you!' A second bolt sped from his fingertips and slammed into the Doctor's body.

The Doctor twisted with the pain but remained standing. He managed a mocking grin. 'Not doing too well, are you?'

Hieronymous hissed with rage and another burst of Helix Energy stabbed the Doctor's chest. This time the pain was excruciating and he fell to one knee. The chain-mail jerkin was taking the force of the impact but growing red-hot in the process and burning into the Doctor's flesh. The Doctor's right hand groped for the wire running to the ground by his side. It too was fiercely hot and on the point of melting. Once that snapped the massive charge of Helix Energy would no longer be 'earthed' and the next bolt would travel directly through the Doctor's body, burning him to a frazzle as it did so.

The Doctor raised his head and looked towards Hieronymous. Surely the Helix Energy was beginning to dwindle? His whole gamble rested on the assumption of a limited, finite amount within each of the brethren. Exhaust it and nothing would remain.

Hieronymous raised his arm a third time and pointed at the Doctor. 'Now die! Now!'

A blue flash of lightning crackled from his fingers but this time not so powerfully, and the impact barely jolted the Doctor. He struggled to his feet and presented his chest squarely towards the advancing Hieronymous. As he did so he felt the earth-wire snap. This was it. He would have to absorb the force of the next bolt himself—or die in the attempt.

'Come on then,' braved the Doctor. Hieronymous raised his arms to the roof and cried out in beseeching tones. 'Mandragora! Help me!' Then, swinging round for the final time he aimed his crooked fingers at the Doctor's chest and let out a piercing vengeful howl. The Doctor closed his eyes as the flash of blue spat through the air towards him.

12

The Final Eclipse

Outside the palace, San Martino lay still and deserted beneath the clear night air. The strong moon light, which earlier had bathed the narrow cobbled streets in a pale silver glow, was now fading as the giant shadow of the Earth crept across the lunar landscape.

Occasionally the sound of music and dancing carried across the rooftops, like distant fairy revels; while beneath the palace walls stood scores of black-hooded brethren, silent and expectant, the shadowy harbingers of death and destruction.

Inside, the masque was in full swing. The guests seemed to have forgotten their earlier anxieties and the wine and music flowed faster and faster. Sarah was even beginning to master the complicated dances, particularly when Giuliano was her partner. But, unlike Cinderella, she kept a firm eye on the clock.

'Have you seen the Doctor?' she panted as Giuliano took hold of her for another gavotte.

'Not yet.'

'It's nearly nine. Something must have happened to him.'

Giuliano gave her hand a reassuring squeeze. 'He may be already here. If he's wearing his costume ...'

'He'd have let us know.' Sarah did a graceful pirouette and at that precise moment caught sight of a lion mask staring at her from the far end of the room behind the dais. She broke off from Giuliano and pushed her way towards it. 'Doctor! What happened? Where have you been?'

The costumed figure gave her a mock salute and whirled away behind a column and into an antechamber.

Sarah caught up with him. 'Stop playing the fool! Tell me what happened!' She stopped herself and stared at the lion's head. There was something different about it. Perhaps she had made a mistake. 'Doctor, it is you ... ?'

The lion's head remained motionless, it's fanged jaws gaping at her in mock derision. She stretched out her hand and quickly pulled the mask off. The shock of what she saw made her scream in terror. No face, no head, nothing, except a dazzling iridescent sphere of light, framed by the cowl of the brethren.

The figure pushed her aside and rushed into the ballroom. From a commanding position on the dais it raised a gloved hand above the heads of the dancing throng and cried out, 'Kill, brothers! Kill!'

There was a curious, unreal silence as the music ceased and everybody looked round. Then pandemonium broke out. People ran in all directions, screeching and yelling with fear. But as the crowd jostled and fought to escape, masked figures within their midst turned upon them with bolts of fire. The goat-head, the oxen, and the grinning clown threw off their headpieces to reveal the familiar cowled shapes of the brethren beneath. Mercilessly, they raised their fingers to shoot blinding, sizzling shafts into the screaming bodies round them. Sarah saw her Florentine gallant hurled to the floor and in seconds the air was thick with the smell of burning flesh. As servants and princes alike dashed for the exits still more brethren poured into the room. In horror Sarah realised they had been let into the palace by their fellows on a given signal. A total massacre seemed imminent.

Suddenly a voice rang out above the din. 'Stop! Stop, brothers!'

Sarah whirled round. On the raised dais stood the commanding form of Hieronymous, in purple cloak and golden mask. He raised his arms above the cowed revellers. The brethren turned, confused.

'The final sacrifices must be made in our temple! Bring the victims of Mandragora down by the temple.'

There was a moment's uncertainty and then Sarah was roughly grabbed by arms of steel and herded into the centre of the room together with the rest. She found herself next to a dazed Giuliano.

He shook his head mournfully. 'The brethren. We

have been tricked, betrayed.'

'Silence!' ordered the figure of Hieronymous. 'Go below, all of you!'

The guests were quickly surrounded by the brethren who made them file out of the palace and into the night towards the ruined temple. As she stumbled over the cobbles in the cold air Sarah wondered despairingly what had befallen the Doctor. Although she hoped against hope, in her heart she knew he must already be dead.

The frightened and bewildered band of captives were marched swiftly through the streets of the city and into the creepy passages of the catacombs. Once assembled in the central sacrificial chamber they were bound with thick rope and grouped in a circle in the ruins about fifty feet from the altar. Sarah had counted twenty heads of state and noblemen amongst the prisoners besides a large number of courtiers of both sexes. The women clung together weeping and moaning, their gay and colourful costumes now torn and mud-spattered by the journey. Giuliano and Marco were roped close together and Sarah was not far away. She thought the young Duke looked defeated and forlorn but his face only expressed what they were all feeling.

The brethren had gathered in a circle round the altar, like a ring of grinning fiends from hell. From out of the shadows the majestic figure of Hieronymous appeared. He ascended the altar steps and lifted his arms up high.

'The eclipse,' whispered Sarah. 'It must be starting.'

Hieronymous's voice echoed loudly round the cavernous chamber. 'Now Mandragora swallows the moon. Now, as it was written, the power of Mandragora will flood the Earth.'

118

There was an eerie grinding noise all around them and Sarah felt a chill wind rustle her hair. The atmosphere was weird, uncanny, devilish. The cracked and jagged walls of the chamber began to shimmer and a strange luminous glow appeared on them. It gradually grew in strength until the outline of a ghostly Roman temple was discernible. At the same time the sound of tumbling masonry was augmented by a high-pitched wail which almost drowned Hieronymous.

'Mandragora, we, your servants welcome you. Bestow your power upon us that we may rule over the whole of your dominion!'

The shrieking, roaring din grew unbearable and Sarah and the other captives buried their heads in one another's shoulders to escape the ear-splitting wail.

Then, a brilliant sphere of light seemed to swoop down through the roof of the temple. It hovered a few moments above the altar then slowly descended into the slab causing it to glow with white-hot heat.

Hieronymous lowered his arms and pointed towards the centre of the altar. The brethren followed suit. There was a hum, like a build-up of power, and suddenly sheets of blue flame leapt from the altar to the outstretched fingers of the encircling brethren. At this instant Hieronymous jumped clear of the altar steps and ran from the central area. But the brethren remained transfixed to the floor, each brother illuminated like a fire-brand with crackling, sizzling Helix Energy. Screams of torture and anguish rang out from the hooded figures as they struggled to move but they seemed held in the grip of an immutable current. Their cloaks caught fire and the ground where they stood erupted with sheets of flame which sped underfoot towards the base of the altar. As the circuit was completed there was a blinding flash and tumultuous explosion. Sarah was hurled to the ground together with everyone around her.

When she recovered the noise and ghostly vision were gone. All that remained was the smoking slab of the sacrificial block where once she had lain herself. Of the entire brethren there was no sign. They had perished where they stood, every single one. All that remained were heaps of empty clothing in a circle round the altar.

Hieronymous mounted the altar steps and took off his mask. Beneath it was revealed the smiling face of the Doctor.

Sarah gasped unable to believe her eyes. 'Doctor!'

The Doctor threw back the purple hood and gazed round at the vanished brethren. 'Even I have to admit that was rather clever of me,' he beamed. Then, taking a breath, he spoke in deep, grating tones the exact replica of Hieronymous's voice.

'A case of energy squared. It puts Mandragora back to square one.'

Sarah stared at him mute with wonder. Giuliano and Marco were likewise struck dumb.

'Well, don't just stand there,' said the Doctor with a touch of impatience. 'I'm ready to accept your congratulations.' He winked at Giuliano. 'I wouldn't even say no to a salami sandwich.'

A day later the Doctor and Sarah were riding across the Slopes of Sorrow to the vineyard where the TARDIS had first landed. Sarah was still numbed by the events of the previous night, but at least she had made the Doctor explain what had happened. His talent for mimicry was self-evident. She had forgotten how gifted he was at such parlour tricks. But his confrontation with Hieronymous was another matter. He explained how he had managed to withstand the astrologer's final desperate onslaught. Once drained of his Helix Energy the outward shape of Hieronymous simply collapsed, like his fellows later. The Doctor had then borrowed his costume to lure the brethren to their destruction.

Now as they jogged across the fields, accompanied by Giuliano and his footman, Sarah felt a deep longing to stay. There was much reparation needed in the hearts and minds of the people of San Martino, and Sarah wanted to share that task with Giuliano. But she knew the Doctor would not understand. He had pulled her leg more than once about the handsome young Duke. Besides, he was already exhibiting signs of itchy feet, and it didn't do to cross him in that mood.

The small group reached the clearing which led to the TARDIS and reined in their horses and dismounted. The Doctor went on ahead to inspect his machine and came back smiling a few minutes later.

'Still there, thank goodness.' He began to munch at an enormous salami sausage. 'Excellent, Giuliano,' he said with his mouth full. 'Thank you.'

The young Duke bowed. 'It is we who should thank you, Doctor. Will you not reconsider?'

'No, we really must be on our way, mustn't we Sarah?'

Sarah gave Giuliano a heartfelt look.

He took her hand. 'There is so much we could learn from you.'

'It will all come in time,' replied the Doctor, a trifle off-hand. 'Keep an open mind, that's all you need.' He shook hands with Giuliano and headed for the TARDIS.

Sarah bit her lip. The Doctor was always the same when it came to saying goodbye, unsentimental and unromantic.

'Come on, Sarah,' he called out as he reached the TARDIS door.

Sarah turned to Giuliano. 'Goodbye, Giuliano.' She kissed him gently on the cheek and hurried off.

The Duke followed her lithe form as she skipped after the Doctor. She was still wearing the satin gown from the ball and her hair in a chignon. She turned before reaching the TARDIS and waved. He saluted in return and shook his head sadly. There were no girls quite like her in San Martino. Nor would there ever be again.

Sarah caught up with the Doctor.

'I never met Leonardo da Vinci then,' he said reaching for the TARDIS key. 'Perhaps it's just as well, I'd have had to tell him his submarine design was totally impractical.'

But Sarah was not listening. 'Poor Giuliano!' she said. 'He looks so wistful. Will he have any more trouble from Mandragora?'

The Doctor paused on the TARDIS threshold. 'He won't, but Earth will. Their constellation will be in position to try again in another five hundred years.'

'Five hundred years? But that takes us to ...' Sarah did a quick calculation, '... just about the end of the twentieth century!'

The Doctor nodded and disappeared inside the TARDIS. Sarah shrugged, gave a final wave to Giuliano, and followed. The door closed behind her.

Twenty yards away Giuliano watched with amazement as the strange blue box began to emit a peculiar trumpeting noise like a wounded animal. Simultaneously, the little white light on top started flashing and the whole contraption slowly faded into thin air before his very eyes.

The footman struggled to control the plunging horses as Giuliano ran forward and probed the ground where the TARDIS had rested. It was just as if nothing had ever been there. The young Duke gazed up at the sky, puzzled, but not afraid.

'There is a reason for everything,' he said to himself. 'Even this. One day science will explain it all.'

'DOCTOR WHO'

0426119657	Doctor Who and The Deadly Assassin	85p
042620042X	Doctor Who – Death to the Daleks	£1.25
0426200969	Doctor Who and the Destiny of the Daleks	90p

IAN MARTER

0426201264	Doctor Who and The Enemy of the World	95p

TERRANCE DICKS

0426112792	Doctor Who and The Giant Robot	95p
0426112601	Doctor Who and The Genesis of the Daleks	95p
0426201310	Doctor Who and The Horns of Nimon	85p
0426200098	Doctor Who and The Horror of Fang Rock	95p
0426200934	Doctor Who and The Invasion of Time	95p
0426200543	Dr Who and The Invisible Enemy	£1.25
0426201485	Doctor Who and The Keeper of Traken	£1.25

PHILIP HINCHCLIFFE

0426201256	Doctor Who and The Keys of Marinus	85p

DAVID FISHER

0426201477	Doctor Who and The Leisure Hive	£1.25

TERRANCE DICKS

0426110412	Doctor Who and The Loch Ness Monster	85p

Prices are subject to alteration

STAR Books are obtainable from many booksellers and newsagents. If you have any difficulty please send purchase price plus postage on the scale below to:-

Star Cash Sales
P.O. Box 11
Falmouth
Cornwall
OR
Star Book Service,
G.P.O. Box 29,
Douglas,
Isle of Man,
British Isles.

While every effort is made to keep prices low, it is sometimes necessary to increase prices at short notice. Star Books reserve the right to show new retail prices on covers which may differ from those advertised in the text or elsewhere.

Postage and Packing Rate

UK: 45p for the first book, 20p for the second book and 14p for each additional book ordered to a maximum charge of £1.63. BFPO and EIRE: 45p for the first book, 20p for the second book, 14p per copy for the next 7 books thereafter 8p per book. Overseas: 75p for the first book and 21p per copy for each additional book.